CW00548858

TREASURED BY 3

Age Gap Dark Mafia Reverse Harem Romance

Three For Me

Book 7

BARBI COX

Copyright © 2023 by Barbi Cox

All rights reserved.

No part of this book may be reproduced in any form or by any electronic or mechanical means, including information storage and retrieval systems, without written permission from the author, except for the use of brief quotations in a book review.

Copyright © 2023 by Barbi Cox

All rights reserved.

No part of this book may be reproduced in any form or by any electronic or mechanical means, including information storage and retrieval systems, without written permission from the author, except for the use of brief quotations in a book review.

ONE

Hunter

I HIT THE PUNCHING BAG. IT'S BEEN A QUIET SIX
weeks. Quiet isn't good, not in our line of work.
Our scouts have found no traces of the Italian
mafia rearing their head again. The low level gangs
are falling in line under Chase's new initiative, that
we can be friends as long as we stay out of each
other's businesses and innocents are spared. As long
as they agree to that and hold each other account-
able, we won't step in and make trouble.

There's been no need for fighting. No need for
hard decisions. So there's nothing for me to do and
I've never felt more useless. The last thing I did was
call both venues Valerie's approved and set up view-
ings. We narrowed down a caterer and Valerie
wants to go cake tasting this week, but we need a
venue to take care of everything else. The décor
Valerie's left to Roger and us. She doesn't care. She

just wants us ... and no goldfish, which is a fad that results in a lot of dead fish at the end of the night–not exactly romantic.

I kick the bag for good measure, then pant before hitting again. It moves back against me, making me jump back. I punch it, but it swings back harder. When I go to hit it again, it moves. I drop my arms and sigh. "Chase, I'm not in the mood for you to-"

Valerie appears, standing in front of the bag and wrapping her arms around it so she can rest against it. She looks me over as I bite the tape around my fists to undo it. "Hi, Dorogaya."

"You've been down here for so long, Krolik. I figured a slow week would be a hot week," she hints.

I roll my eyes at her, but she steps forward and rubs over my sweaty chest. She writes "I love you" there and stretches on her toes. I press a kiss to her soft lips. "Hit the bag, Valerie."

She glances at it, punches it and faces me. "I'm off work. Why don't we go on a date?"

I nod once. "Sure. That sounds good."

She wraps her arms around me. "We can go make out in a movie theater, we can go on some crazy wild date where you can spoil me, or we can have a movie marathon so you can tell me every-thing wrong with mafia movies."

Sighing, I press my forehead to hers. "You know me too well."

"And not well enough at the same time," she says in disagreement. "Chase is doing the mafia boss thing. Lief is doing ... Lief things. Let's do something together, just us. It's been a long time since we've done that."

"Two weeks," I say, tapping her temple. "How badly was your head rattled again?"

"That's too long for us. Last time you bought out a whole movie theater," she says.

"Because I'm the only one who gets to hear you come," I answer.

She blushes at the memory. "That poor usher."

"There was no permanent damage, and I warned them not to come in until after the credits. He didn't listen." I shrug.

"That doesn't mean scaring the hell out of a teenager just for seeing me riding you. I still had ... most of my clothes on." She blushes and bites her bottom lip.

I groan and lift her up. Valerie wraps her legs around me as I kiss her. "You keep making that face and we will not make it out of this room."

"Maybe I want to take you ax throwing ... or see you beat up some people at a gym," she pants against my lips. "Seeing you in action, knowing you can't be killed ... it drives me wild."

I groan. "Then I'm taking you to the best fucking restaurant in the entire city, and we're going to my club."

"The sexy one?" she asks.

I grin. "Yes. The sexy one. I'll let you mingle, wait for some asshole to make his move and either get turned on watching you kick him in the balls and threaten him with a knife, or you'll get turned on by watching me break a hand."

She shudders. "Or we fuck in one of those private rooms."

"You're so damn ... perfect for me," I growl against her mouth before kissing her hard.

"And tomorrow, we're going to look at a venue," she says before biting my bottom lip. "Where we can say 'I do'."

"Yeah, we're not going to make it through dinner," I say.

She squeals, tries to escape me, but we just end up having a quicky in the shower. We end up changed and I just stare at Valerie. I love watching her get dressed. Especially when 'dressed' means a skimpy little red dress that barely covers her ass and hugs her curves. I groan when she slides into heels.

"I'm going to have to blind so many people today," I say in a low growl.

"Is that a compliment or a warning to change?" she asks, sassy as ever before, tracing her lips in a dark red, darker than any wine. I bet I'd get twice as drunk on it. She arches an eyebrow. "Hunter?"

"I'd never tell you to change. I'd never tell you to put on more clothes. I'll just take care of anyone who tries to touch you, photograph you, carry you away," I say. "You're sexy as hell, and I love how you own it."

Valerie blinks at me a few times, then she's in my arms, on top of me. She kisses me passionately and I grab her ass. She rubs herself against me, feasting on my mouth. I draw back and moan, catching her wrists before she can go for my pants. I flip her over and hold her down.

"Oh, no you don't. You're not getting out-of-date night," I say in warning. "You have to be a good girl."

"In which way? You love when I'm naughty. Isn't that considered good?" she asks.

I chuckle. "You're going to behave like the lady I know you are when we're in public and be my naughty minx in private."

Valerie whines in her throat. She draws back and I get off her. I adjust my suit jacket, then look at myself in the mirror. No lipstick on me. I touch my mouth and Valerie giggles. "Do you think I'd take a chance on anything that would smear around you three? You can't keep your hands or mouths off me."

I pull her close, then look her over. "Will you be warm, or should we go shopping?"

"You planned a gorgeous date. Keep planning. I lovc you taking initiative," she croons.

"We're shopping first," I decide.

That's what we do. I pull out one of my nice

cars, get Valerie in the passenger side, and take her to the most expensive stretch of road in the city. She rolls her eyes, but doesn't argue when I lead her into an exclusive boutique.

The attendants take one look at me and jump to attention. I wrap my arm around Valerie's waist. "My girlfriend needs a coat, a good one, that matches her dress."

"Of course!" Two of them hurry around, presenting options while one brings us champagne.

Valerie sips. I take my glass and nod. "Also, something sexy that will fit under that dress without showing, a pair of gloves, and what do you think, Dorogaya? Do you need boots?"

"There's no snow, so I'm okay in heels. Although, I think if they had a garter belt and thigh highs," Valerie hints.

I touch my chest. "I love you."

"I know you, Hunt, I know what you like," she purrs in Russian.

I pull her tighter and kiss her just below her ear. After I turn down a few coats, some that are fur, others that just don't work, we find a black leather coat that's fashionable, sexy, and perfect. I nod to it. Someone shows a black garter belt that's more like a see through, high wasted skirt. Before Valerie hurries away with another attendant, I'm shown a few gloves and choose a good faux-fur lined leather pair.

Valerie returns. I get my bill as she pulls on the coat and I stick her gloves in her pocket. I lead her back to the car and drag her across the seat to kiss her. I nip at her bottom lip and run my tongue over the same place. "You drive me insane. What lingerie do you have on?"

"Be a good boy and you'll find out," she teases.

I take her to the most expensive, experimental, amazing restaurant in the city. It's booked out months in advance, but when I walk in, I get the next table available and I glower at the couple that disagrees. Valerie takes off her coat and the man can't help but stare. I snap my fingers at him.

"You brought a beautiful woman here and you're ignoring her for mine? You should reconsider," I advise him.

The woman he's with huffs. "I knew it. I knew you weren't into me anymore. Did you bring me here to break up with me?"

"No!" he exclaims, following her out.

Valerie shakes her head as I pull her back. "We need to work on how you word things."

"I didn't punch him," is all I answer.

She giggles and laughs throughout the meal, shocked at the fusion of science and food. It's an experience, even if the food isn't up to my standards. Getting personal time with Valerie is worth subpar food.

I tip a decent amount, loop my arm with

Valerie's, and then we're back in the car. I drive over the speed limit until Valerie digs her nails into my thigh. I glance at her and don't see even a bit of a smile on her face. She glowers. "Slow. Down."

"Really?"

"Now!"

I let off the gas. She shakes her head. "You're going to get yourself killed."

"I'd never be reckless with you in the car," I argue.

"You were going 110!" she argues. "I want you conscious, alive, and present on our wedding day."

"I will be!" I insist. "I'm not being reckless."

"Don't ... don't be so fast, Hunter. I worry that you're going to hit something or someone will hit you," Valerie insists. "If I unbuckled right now-"

"You'd wouldn't dare," I growl.

"Speed again and find out," she dares.

I narrow my eyes, and her hand goes to the buckle. We have a mild standoff, but I stay within a reasonable speed and she stays buckled until I park at the club. I walk around the side of the car and let her out. "I'll stay under the speed limit out there, but once we get to bed..."

"Now you have to work me up. The thought of you getting hurt is the opposite of a turn on. My switch is set to off," she says as we walk in.

She takes off her coat and, without looking back at me, walks right onto the dance floor. I glower at the manager and he immediately prepares the V.I.P.

section as I go to reclaim my woman. By the time I get to her, a guy already has his hand around her waist. I narrow my eyes at him. Valerie spots me, turns, and glowers at the man.

He's fucked and doesn't even know it.

TWO

Valerie
_____

"Get off me now. I'm not single. I'm not available. I don't want you on me," I hiss.

He puts his hands up. "You didn't seem to mind when I was grinding on you a second ago. Maybe your man is forgettable."

"Fuck off," I grunt, before turning around to walk to Hunter.

The asshole grabs my trailing arm and tugs me back. I narrow my eyes at him. "You're making a mistake. You're not my type. I promise you that."

"I've seen you in the news, baby. I know you want more than one man. How about two?" the guy asks as another grinds on me.

Glancing back, I see another stranger. "Oh, we can take good care of you."

I sigh. "I was trying to have a nice date night. You're either the on switch, or you're going to eat your teeth. Choose."

He laughs. "You're fierce."

The other guy gropes my ass. Well. This is going to get Hunter hot, and I know he's not fond of anyone touching me. It's a miracle that everyone who's seen me naked isn't dead with his level of possession/ protectiveness. I ignore the ass grabber and pull my recent gift from Lief on the guy in front of me. I hear it slice through his jeans and grin. Lief made it extra sharp.

The guy pales as he looks down. "What are…."

"Oh, that's not my hand, *sweetheart*. Want to know how sharp I keep my knives, or are you ready to move on?" I snarl. "Your buddy's getting his hand broken in a second either way."

"You only have two hands. One hand off me and we're going to have some fun," he grunts.

I laugh. "It's cute that you think your two inches could satisfy me after so much big talk."

I see Hunter closing in. He grabs the guy's hand off my ass and I glance back, watching as he breaks the guy's wrist with a simple twist. The asshole yells just as the music crescendos. He drops to his knees, clutching his hand.

Hunter takes his spot and kisses my neck. "Are you playing nice?"

"No," I answer. "I thought the owner of the club would have more popularity here."

The stranger looks between me and Hunter. "You … you own.."

I glower at him. "You're talking to *me*. Do you

want to keep your balls or give them to me as an early wedding present?"

He holds his hands up. "Keep them. Sounds like the best option."

He hurries away. Hunter twirls me under his arm and pulls me back against him. "God, I love watching you pull a knife on people."

I drag it up his chest, over the buttons, and watch them pop off. Hunter watches me with so much lust and eagerness in his eyes. I put the flat side against his neck and arch an eyebrow. "Think I can take you?"

"Do you want to try?" Hunter asks.

I grin and move my hand ever so slightly, just for Hunter to grab my wrist, dig his finger into it, between my tendons, so I drop the knife. He spins me and pulls me flush against him, so he's grinding against my ass with his hand around my throat.

"Naughty, naughty girl," he growls in my ear, low and threatening. "You know I have to punish you for what you did to my shirt and for pulling a knife on me. What kind of mafia boss would I be if I let that go?"

"Punish me then ... if you can," I dare him.

Hunter drags me to a private room. He slams the door and tosses me on a bed. Before I can get my bearings, he's on top of me. He shows me the knife he picked up at some point and slices my dress off me. I pant. "Hunt, how can I ..."

"Don't you worry about the how," he says

before looking over my lingerie. It's not even close to classy. No one would call it that, but Hunter looks at me as if he can't get enough, as if he simply *needs* me. "Fucking ... Valerie, I need to marry you faster."

"I know what you like, Krolik," I agree.

He rips it off me like a kid on Christmas, so overjoyed and starving for me and he can't wait the extra seconds it would take to remove the fabric. Then he flips me over, spreads my legs, and licks over my pussy while spanking me. I whimper, moan, and rock back against him.

His tongue knows me far too well. He sucks my clit while spanking me hard. The mix of pleasure and pain makes me dizzy. Just as I'm about to come for him, he stops. I whine. "Hunter!"

"It wouldn't be a punishment if I didn't make you whine," he says, chuckling with another slap to my ass.

Then he's inside me, big, thick, and fucking perfect. My eyes roll back and I almost come from that alone. Hunter grabs my hair, jerking me up until I'm almost riding him, but he grabs my throat instead and strokes down my body, teasing my nipples.

"What will be worse for you, having your nipples played with, or your clit before I deny you again?" he asks.

"Both," I pant.

"Liar," he growls before tightening his hold on

my throat and pounding into me like a jackhammer. It's so damn good, so perfect, so ... my eyes roll back as my core spasms around him. Hunter stops, just stops, with the tip of his cock still inside me.

I huff. "Hunter Volkov, if you don't fuck me properly, I'm going to do it myself while you watch!"

He laughs and bites my throat hard. I moan and shudder as he swats my clit. "You naughty girl."

Pushing me down to my elbows, he holds me in place, one firm hand on my upper back as he slams into me again and again. He keeps swatting my ass. "I'm going to have to break you. Going to remind you to be sweet to me."

"Sweet isn't what you like," I say.

"From you I do," he snarls, stopping again.

It's torture in the best way. The constant intensity, then nothingness. Never knowing when he's going to stop, if he's going to let me come this time, it's too much. I whimper as he spins me again. My ass hurts.

"Please, Hunter. Please! Hunt. I need to come. I need to come for you. I'm too ... it's too much! I can't wait, Hunter, please!"

"God, your begging is so damn good," he groans, jerking me back against him. "How can I resist?"

"Come with me," I beg. "I want you to come too!"

He groans and comes down on top of me, his

hands on mine, kissing my neck, my chin, then my lips as he fucks meme, thrusting in and out slowly, letting me feel every inch of him. He's everywhere, everything, and I've never loved being submissive more than right now.

Hunter groans against my lips, and I come. My eyes flutter and then roll back. "Hunter!"

"Fuck, keep coming, Dorogaya. Even more. Enjoy every second of it," he orders me while rubbing my clit in fast circles.

I can't come down. There's just too much pleasure, pure ecstasy made all the better by the wait for it. Hunter groans, rocks his hips against me again, then collapses with me. We pant together as he strokes my side and kisses the back of my neck and shoulder. He licks the bite mark I'm sure he's left.

"I love you," I pant.

He rubs my ass. "I love you so much. And you were right."

I roll under him and he moves to lie next to me. I swallow. "I was right about what?"

"I do like when you're naughty with me, when you're vicious and sharp and ... perfect," he answers before kissing me. "We need to go out more."

"You just enjoyed hurting someone," I snort.

"Not as much as I liked you putting someone in their place and everything that happened after," he says, chuckling.

I snuggle against him. The music fades away.

It's just us, where we should be. A few minutes later, there's a knock on the door.

"Occupied!" Hunter yells.

"Yeah, yeah. I'm not a delivery boy," Lief says while opening the door. He looks at me. His jaw tightens as his thick, blonde hair falls over his shoulder. Blue eyes have never looked so warm. "Valerie."

"Hi, Viking. I like the present you got me. Knives are good," I say while biting my thumb.

"For you, not other people," Hunter says as he pulls on his boxers and pants. Lief walks over to me as Hunter shuts the door.

Lief cups my face in his hand. "I'm offended I wasn't invited."

"You were busy," I say. "You and Chase. Plus, if you were by my side, I wouldn't have gotten all hot and heavy with Hunt."

Lief lifts my chin and kisses me. I melt against him and pull him closer. I'm happy to have him too. Right here and now. Hunter sighs. "I'll get us some liquor. Have fun."

Lief climbs on top of me, jerking the shreds of my dress away from my body. "We're going on a date soon."

"Yes, Viking," I sigh as he cups my breast and circles his thumb around my nipple. "Soon."

"Very soon. Tomorrow," he says, deciding before kissing me again, long and deep kisses, so perfect and amazing that I want to dissolve into him. I tug on his shirt, but he catches my hand. He holds his lips a millimeter away so I can feel every word, but can't kiss him. "You're not fucking me until then."

"That sounds like a challenge," I purr, moving closer and spreading my legs.

He sucks in a breath and shakes his head, handing me the bag. "Dressed."

"Lief," I whine.

He kisses me again. I'm so dizzy from his mouth on mine, his light touches, that I don't realize he's dressing me until we part and he jerks a dress over my head and forces my arms through. I pout. "But-"

He dangles panties from his finger.

I look from him to the panties. "Maybe you should put them on. I don't know if they're comfortable. Try it, Viking."

"I'd rip them. Yes or no?" he asks.

I take them and shimmy them on, trying to tempt Lief as much as possible. He flips me and looks at my ass. "We're going to have to ice your butt."

"I guess that means no bath together tonight?" I ask.

He kisses my bottom, then bites. I gasp and make a low mcwling sound as I arch to give him more access. He chuckles and pulls my dress over my ass. "I know you're eager, pet. Let's dance and have some fun. Chase misses you."

"You brought Chase too?" I ask.

"Yes. Let's go enjoy being V.I.P.'S," he says, while pulling me up effortlessly. "It'll be a first for me."

"You're not working?" I ask.

"I'm training only now. I'm no longer security," he says.

I squeal and jump into his arms, hugging him tight. I breathe him in and sigh. "That means so much to me, Lief. It does."

He rubs my back and kisses my temple. "I'm glad. I'm being safe for you."

"He says until someone touches my ass," I tease.

"Who touched your ass?" Lief growls. "I'll ..."

"Hunter already broke their hand. I pulled a knife on the other one. You sharpened it well. It cut right through his jeans."

Lief radiates pride as we get back on the dance floor. I dance with him, then Chase picks me up and spins me. He kisses me and I pull him close. "I've missed you, baby boy. Stop working so much."

"I know. I have all of tomorrow off ... mostly. I'm excited to defile the venues with you, do some cake tasting, and make sure this wedding happens in a few months," Chase says against my mouth.

I kiss him again. My guys and I party like we're all twenty-one. We drink too much, get far too handsy for public, dance and enjoy the club until it closes.

THREE

Chase

I RUB MY FOREHEAD IN THE MORNING. I'M NOT twenty anymore. Not even close. I smell bacon and roll, expecting to have Valerie and Hunter in bed. Nope. I've been cuddling Lief instead of Valerie.

He's so dead to the world that he's snoring. Hunter groans, curses about it being too light, then jerks the curtains closed.

I try to massage the pounding in my head away. "Fuck, how late?"

"Three a.m. ... no. We got some kind of drive through on the way home. My car is still at the club," Hunter groans. "Four ... that's when we got in bed."

I lift the sheet to make sure I still have boxers on. Boxers and my pants ... well, one leg of my pants. Lief's dressed, but is missing a shoe. Hunter's got boxers on. I get up, wave through the nausea, and shake my head.

"Don't get up, loves," Valerie says. "I'm bringing breakfast in bed."

"You're a saint. Saint Valerie," Hunter groans. "But turn down the smile. You're too perky."

"Of course I'm perky, we're going to the venues today and doing cake-tasting!" She almost cheers.

Lief is still completely out. I pick at the toast, take the meds she offers, and the coffee. The more I eat, the better I feel. I can see Hunter feels the same. Then I realize why. There's Irish cream in our coffee.

Hunter sighs. "She is a saint."

I chuckle. Valerie returns with food and coffee for Lief and sighs. "Sleeping beauty."

"You're the one who has to kiss him," I say, edging away from the giant.

Valerie takes that spot and brushes Lief's hair back from his face. She kisses the corner of his mouth, but he doesn't wake. His head turns slightly to the side, and he rubs the spot she kissed. She narrows her eyes.

"Lief, intruder alert!" She yells.

He starts, jumps up, and looks around. He groans and stretches. "Where?"

"You're the intruder. You swatted at my kiss," she says with a pout.

He rubs her cheek. "You don't deserve my morning breath."

She hands him his coffee, and he sighs. "Thank you. That's the best sleep I've had in so long."

"Are you hung over at all?" Hunter demands.

Lief shrugs. "Headaches are normal. I've existed under worse conditions."

It's a miracle that Hunter and I can put ourselves together enough to go to the venues. The first one is nice, I can say that. My father was right about it being easy to secure, but the more Valerie listens, the more I can tell she doesn't like it. She liked the staircases but is not interested in the rest of it.

Hunter shakes his head. "It's not good enough."

I elbow him when the woman glances at us and blushes. Her eyes flick to Lief and she gives him a very thorough once-over. Lief doesn't notice at all. He squints at the sky. "No trees?"

"Well," she says. "Um, there's no guarantee it will be this sunny and most people have the reception inside."

"It's too bright for photos if we're wearing white," he states. "Clouds in spring mean rain, so we're either soaking or burning up."

"We haven't selected a date yet, Viking. We don't know what the weather will be," Valerie answers.

He shrugs, and she wraps her arms around one of his. "How are you feeling?"

"Unimpressed."

That wraps up the first place. I roll my eyes as we're back in the car. "Can either of you be polite or kind while we're going through a venue? It's not the person's job to make sure we like it, it's their job to give us all the details, and that's what she did."

"I didn't comment on her knowledge," Lief says.

"It just wasn't for us," Hunter agrees. "There's nothing insulting about that."

Valerie moves closer and kisses my cheek. "I get it, baby boy. You don't want to make things awkward."

"It might be a good venue for something else in the future. A ball, or something like that. We should maintain a good relationship as business professionals," I insist.

Valerie smiles and kisses me again. "So responsible and mature."

"Hey! I'm the older brother," Hunter argues.

I kiss her back, flipping Hunter off as Valerie gives me her undivided attention. It's no secret they had plenty of fun last night. It shouldn't hurt his feelings that she's giving me a few kisses.

When we pull up to Larz Anderson House, Valerie smiles. I keep her hand and Lief takes the back as Hunter walks on her other side. Every room is gorgeous. The murals on the wall, the walkway with gold accents, then the area they recommend for the reception. There's a small pool, a glass overlay in case of rain, lanterns, and yet, it's beautiful and refined.

Hunter and Lief haven't said a bad word at all. I squeeze Valerie's hand. "What do you think?"

"It's amazing. It's ... I mean, there's something different in every room, but it all matches," she gushes.

"This is a good area for a reception. I like the optional glass covering. There are many areas for photos of us getting ready as well as options for the ceremony," Lief says, pragmatic as ever.

"What dates are available?" Hunter asks.

Valerie gasps. "Are we choosing here?"

"We narrowed it down to two in all of D.C.." Lief shrugs. "A destination wedding will alienate some guests, take more time, preparation, and security. Why would we hesitate?"

"I like it here. I think it gives us everything we need, plus the natural décor," I say in agreement.

Hunter nods. "Sexy and classy, just like you, Dorogaya."

The woman that's been showing us around arches her eyebrows. Valerie bounces. "Yes, earliest dates?"

"Well ... we're normally booked through spring and summer," the woman says. She must read something on Lief's impassive face. She checks a few things and nods. "We did have a cancellation for late April. I don't know if that will be possible for you considering it's already February, but-"

"We'll take it," I say at the same time as Hunter.

"Right, and the bride and groom are?" she asks, flushing as she looks at us.

"All of us. We're right here," Valerie states,

without a trace of worry. "I'm the bride. These three are the grooms. We're thrilled."

"Very ... very well, the deposit is-" she starts.

I hand her my card before Hunter can. She nods again. "One ... just one second, please."

"Asshole, I'm reserving the caterer," Hunter growls.

"No fighting. There are plenty of costs to go around," Valerie insists.

"And next to nothing for you to pay for," Lief says as he pulls her back against him. "You'll be outvoted."

She huffs, but continues looking around. Valerie slips out of a shoe and dips her toes in the water, giggling. "It's perfect. It is. The staircase, the study, the antique windows and luxurious hallways. It's better than a Victorian house."

I take her hand and pull her back from the water. "Are you happy?"

"I'd be happier if we were doing set up now. Oh, I have to get a dress," she whispers.

I glance at Hunter and Lief. Valerie's lips tick down, but she catches it and smiles at us. "That will be fun for Sophie, Danny and me to do."

"Danny?" Hunter asks.

"Oh, that's Sophie's sister-in-law. I've met her a few times, and she's cool. I'll invite Elaine and Josephine ... and Vanya," she nods like that, tics everything off the list.

I meet her eyes, but don't bring up her mother. "What about Tristan?"

"Nope. Girls only," she says, tapping my nose. "But good try, trying to get him to spy."

"You're really going to make us wait until our wedding to see you?" Hunter groans.

Valerie slips back into her shoe. "I am. It's good luck."

"You're killing me," he groans.

"And none of you get to see what I'll be wearing under it until the night of." She wiggles against me until I stop her hips.

Lief grins. "Maybe we'll have to surprise you, too."

She gapes, argues, but the woman returns with my card. "Well, we will see you all at the end of April. Here's the date, my phone number since I'll help coordinate all the décor, the caterer, and everything else. My name is Zoey."

Her eyes go to Lief again and I note the blatant lust there. Compared to the almost immediate turn-off girls get from him, it's kind of strange. Lief nods. "Appreciated."

"Don't hesitate to reach out with any questions, if you need to set up photography sessions, or if you just have any questions," she says in a breathy voice.

Lief just nods once. I swear, the girl nearly comes the second his eyes meet hers. Weird. Hunter's too distracted with our fiancée to notice, and Valerie either doesn't notice or is picking her battles.

We head to the bakery that was highly recommended. Lief scrolls through the reviews. "How many cakes are we eating?"

"We're *tasting* ten cakes. I figure we'll each try two and eliminate, and continue from there. If we don't all like it, there's no reason to have it. Also, I saw this new thing where the top layer is for us and the rest is for the guests, so I think that will be fun. We can make sure that it's a flavor that others will like," Valerie says.

"And we are not doing the cake throwing thing," Hunter says. "I'm sure I'll already be having trouble keeping my hands to myself at the ceremony and reception. I don't need a reason to lick you, Dorogaya."

"Cute to think you'd be the one doing the licking, Krolik," she says, winking at him.

He groans. "I'm fucking you at that venue."

"Agreed," I say in her ear. "I don't care how many layers you wear."

"Are you wearing one dress or two?" Lief asks, still on his tablet.

"What?" we all ask.

He blinks and looks up at us. "Some women purchase a dress for the wedding and one for the reception, one that's lighter and shorter for the reception, so it's easier to move."

Valerie's lips part, then she shuts them. "I'll see if something shorter catches my eye."

We get to the bakery and the cakes are laid out in front of us. They're small slices, thankfully. Hunter grabs the chocolate, but Valerie's eying one that says, caramel almond, Lief grabs the carrot cake and I grab a simple buttercream with a raspberry middle.

Valerie pouts after one bite and gently pushes it away. I rub her thigh. "You don't like it?"

Lief blinks at her as he chews. "You like caramel."

"It's just not the right sweet to not-sweet ratio," she says. "I bet Hunt would like it."

I like the buttercream, and Hunter loves the chocolate. Lief sets the carrot cake to the side and we all choose a second cake. Hunter chews, then turns to me and offers me the fork. "Try this."

"That's not the way-"

"I need to see if you think the same thing as me," he says.

I take a bite. It's like a strawberry milkshake and cake. It's light, the cake is moist, it's delicious. "Strawberry milkshake," I say. "But ... with whipped cream."

Hunter nods. "Exactly! How crazy is that?"

Valerie feeds Lief some frosting on her finger, and his eyes heat. He makes a face and looks at the cake in accusation. "Lemon."

"You don't like sour?" Valerie asks.

"No," his simple reply. Then he feeds her a bite of his. Before she can swallow, he kisses her, then continues down her neck. "It's orange and cocoa."

"It's ... it's good, but I'm biased," she sighs.

We pass the plates around, trying the approved one, but I see Valerie light up for the strawberry one. She touches her mouth and blinks a few times, then lets Lief have a bite. Before she moves on, I see her taste some kind of franken-cake: the strawberry frosting with the chocolate cake.

She moans so deep, licking her lips, that none of us looks away. We fight to have the same taste and just like that, we've settled on a venue and a cake. It's progress in the quiet period, which is more than I dared to hope for.

FOUR

Valerie

Since my last session was canceled, I spend time checking off the wedding things. We decided on the cake and only doing the one we all liked–the guests will love it anyway–and the venue. I know Lief contacted a floral shop to see their orchids and their recommendations for wedding centerpieces featuring them. We have the caterer and sent them the date. We even made the deposit.

We've accomplished so much in a week, but there's still a long list. Choosing the bridesmaids and groomsmen, finding an officiant, getting my wedding dress, getting our rings made, and the big one, the one that's larger than anything else: who am I marrying on paper?

I nibble my bottom lip as I stare at it. I'm still nervous about having the Volkov name tied to me. If I choose Hunter, Chase might be upset. If I choose Chase, Hunter will be upset. But Chase is the Mafia boss, so how can I ignore that? Isn't it expected that I'll marry him? Marrying Lief on paper would be easiest. I'd take his last name, or keep my own. Sure, it doesn't have the same ring as Valerie Volkov, but won't it be safer that way? Not that it's not obvious I'm with them all now.

I groan and drop my head to the desk. I stay like that for a long moment before remembering Sophia was in this position. I call her quickly.

"Hey, I thought you'd still be at work," she answers.

"Want to be my maid of honor?" I ask.

"Yes! I didn't want to put any pressure on you, but of course! I can't wait," Sophia grins before gushing about her wedding day and how meaningful it was.

"Um, I'm going to ask Elaine to be a bride's maid, but how about Danny too? I like her. We text every now and again. Do you think she could make it from Italy?" I ask.

"She would! Massimo loves weddings and I'm sure they'd love to join," Sophia agrees.

We talk a bit more about the plans, but then she pauses. I check the connection and she sighs. "What's wrong?"

"What do you mean?"

"I can hear the smile fading off your face. What's wrong?" she insists.

"How did you pick who you'd marry on paper? How'd you decide whose last name to take?" I ask.

"Well, Holden and Nick weren't demanding in that respect. They told me having me was more than enough. Gunner was eager, but it was the *one* thing Roman asked for when it came to the wedding. It was the only thing that mattered to him. He wanted to be my legal husband, and he wanted me to take his name. I was happy to do it," she explains. "Are the guys fighting over it?"

"I'm just anxious. I mean, the Volkov name carries such weight and if I marry Hunter on paper, Chase will be offended. If I marry Chase on paper, Hunter will pout. I think marrying Lief would fix all that and then I could keep my name, but everyone expects me to marry the mafia boss, so Chase still has to be considered and I-"

"The what?" Sophia asks, her voice stoic. I can picture her face, lips parted, eyes wide, confused beyond being able to yell.

I rewind my mind and realize what I said. I groan. "They're going to kill me for outing them."

"I'm on my way. Right now. Hold, get the plane ready!" Sophie yells.

"I wasn't being serious, they're not going to-"

"See you soon. A few hours max. I'll kick some ass," she says before hanging up.

I sigh and massage my temples. Great. Trying to get some help resulted in opening a huge can of worms. I hinted to Chase that I wanted to tell her, but that's different than doing it. I didn't talk to

Hunter or Lief about it. There was no agreement in place.

"Just breathe," I tell myself as my hands shake. "You know how to deal with anxiety attacks. Just breathe and ground yourself."

I rub my desk and the fabric of my chair. It brings my rational brain to the front. I'm in my office. I'm safe. I can handle this. I'm planning a wedding with the men I love. I faced down someone with a gun weeks ago. I can handle telling my men I slipped and told Sophia. Chase said that Holden already knows. So the family can keep a secret.

Glancing at the time, I realize my shift is over. Well, better to deal with it right away and not let it drag out. I'll just get more anxious until it bursts out of me and I can't have that. So I go right to the mansion.

The security guy stops me, looks at me, and smiles. "Valerie! How nice to see you! Are you on the schedule?"

"Do I need to be?" I ask.

He hesitates. "Well, Mr. Volkov has limited who can come in, but I guess it's assumed you're included with them now."

"That is assumed," I say, flashing my engagement rings.

His eyes dip to them and he nods. "Yes, I'll let Mr. Volkov know you're on your way."

"Which one?" I ask.

"Ch-Chase," he says, stumbling over the word

before muttering in Russian about how wrong it is to call him that.

Soon enough, I'm parked and staring at the mansion as it stares back. I promised them way back when that I'd never tell what they did. Even when I was ready to leave them, I never planned to share their secret. Ever. Even on pain of death, unless I knew they were coming.

Taking a deep breath, I narrow my eyes at the mansion. No building is going to intimidate me. I walk in, summoning all the confidence I have, and walk into the conference room. Chase is there alone. He glances at his watch.

"I only have ten minutes before a very important meeting," he says, adjusting his shirt.

God, he's attractive. Wearing slacks and a button up pushed to his elbows, a few buttons undone, so formal and proper, his glasses low on his nose. He's like a sexy professor, or some nerdy accountant and holy shit, I can't stand it.

I slam the door, walk to him, and shove him back so he's sitting on the table. He gasps. "Valerie!"

I kiss him, devouring his moan as our tongues tease and tangle. He strokes my sides, squeezing me against him. I rub myself on him, pulling on his shirt and undoing buttons until I can touch his chest and abs.

Chase groans as I kiss his neck. He takes a ragged breath. "This is why you came?"

"It wasn't, but I ... I can't help it. You look so sexy, baby boy," I groan.

He tangles his fingers in my hair, pulling back as I pant. I nod and stroke him through his pants. "Be rough with me right here in the conference room before you dominate it."

"Fuck," he rasps before kissing me again, spinning us and laying me across the table. He bunches my skirt around my hips and groans against my mouth. I pull at my shirt, jerking it over my breasts. Chase draws back to watch as he drags my bra down to kiss and suck my nipple. I gasp and arch my back.

"Yes, just like that! So good," I moan.

I pull at his belt, and he pulls himself out. I nod to his cock. "Please!"

"You want my cock? Are you sure you're wet enough?" He asks.

"Please," I beg again.

Chase pushes my knees to my chest and licks over my pussy. He moves up and down, his shoulders bobbing as he keeps his tongue flat from my entrance to my clit again and again until I'm writhing against him.

"Chase!"

"Tell me why you came here and I'll let you come," he says, bartering.

"Make me come and I'll tell you ... while making you come," I offer instead.

He groans and sucks my clit until I want to cry

with pleasure. He twists his tongue, curls it, then just flicks across the sensitive bud until I can't keep my eyes open. I hold my legs in place, clawing myself.

I fall over the edge, moaning and yelling his name as I come. My legs fall slack as my hands slip. Chase moans and taps his cock against my clit. "Tell me, naughty girl. I want to know."

"Please, I need your cock," I beg. "Please, baby boy. I need you filling me, fucking me. Just you."

He bends over me, grabbing the nape of my neck. "Just me?" he demands.

"Yes!" I whine. "Just you, fucking me until the whole mansion knows how much I love you, how crazy you make me. Please!"

Chase groans and fills me. My lips part and I curl towards him, my lips brushing his. He groans with me and kisses me hard. Our tongues brush until my eyes roll back and I claw his shoulders, pulling myself closer so I can kiss his collarbone, his shoulder, everything I can reach. He pounds into me hard.

"You're so damn wicked," he snarls. "Destroying my plans."

"So good. You're so good to me, baby boy. Don't stop. I love your cock. I love *you*," I moan.

He grunts. "Fuck, Valerie, I ..."

I roll my hips against him and he fucks me harder, deeper. The slight curve to his cock rubs me so that I swear I see sparkles instead of the lights.

My head falls back and Chase bites my neck hard, right in the front.

"Mine," he snarls. "All mine."

"Yes! Yes!" I chant. "Chase, don't stop!"

He groans and reaches between us, rubbing my clit. He smears my wetness over my nipple and sucks hard as we get louder and louder. It's stupid to think that the security right outside the door doesn't hear us, but it just makes it better. I tug his hair, demanding his mouth and taste myself there.

My other hand grabs his ass, nails digging in, just like he enjoys. Chase jerks back, flips me over, then fucks me from behind, massaging my breast in one hand as he jackhammers into me. He's ferocious, ruthless, amazing.

He tugs my hair back. "I didn't say to be quiet."

Chase spanks me hard until I'm mewling and moaning, unable to control how loud I am or what falls out of my mouth. He grunts and growls behind me before biting my shoulder. "Come!"

I whimper and rub my clit, sliding my fingers around him until he trembles. "Fucking come, baby doll, or you're going to be upset."

I moan and my body gives in as my legs give out. I tremble and pant as I lose myself in the ecstasy Chase gives. My vision dims as I pant around the raspy sounds leaving my throat. Chase doesn't pull out. He comes deep inside me, shaking as he grinds into my pussy.

After one more moan and shiver, I flop to the

table, spent. "I should come here more often after work."

Chase swats my ass and kisses the back of my neck. "I like your surprises."

I hum and smile. We put ourselves back together and Chase checks the time. "Why are you here again, baby doll?"

I open my mouth to tell him, but Lief walks in. He arches an eyebrow at me, then shuts the door. "Sir, your guests-"

"I told Sophia that you're the mafia boss," I say, so I can't put it off.

Chase and Lief both stare at me with a mix of horror, anger, and shock. I suck my bottom lip as I curl in on myself.

FIVE

Lief

I don't know how to react. Valerie was never supposed to tell anyone. Not a soul. Ever. I'm sure we had that conversation, but even if we hadn't, it was understood. We're to be businessmen and nothing more.

Worse still, we can't have a conversation about it because the heads from the other branches are here to meet with Chase, welcome him in, and congratulate him on his upcoming marriage. They've been happy to forget that Hunter and I are a part of the deal.

"Let me see what the holdup is," Hunter says in Russian from outside the door. He opens it, sees how Chase is puffing up in front of Valerie, and closes the door with a quick, "one minute."

Valerie whimpers. "I didn't mean to. I called Soph with a simple wedding question or two and it just ... it fell out while I was explaining something and-"

"You told her. You said you'd talk to us first," Chase hisses.

"Talk to us about what?" Hunter asks.

Valerie cringes as she looks between us. She hugs Chase. "I know it was wrong. I'm sorry. I wish I could take it back, but I can't. She's on her way."

Valerie tries to scurry away, but I catch her and level her with my gaze. "You were planning to do this?"

"I mean, Sophia's noticed I've been keeping something from her. She brought it up at our engagement party. She was sure that I wasn't telling her everything when the news broke about me and Yuri, but I told Chase-"

"What did you tell her?" Hunter demands.

Valerie turns around, keeping her back right against me. "I told Sophia what you guys do. It was in passing. A mention, but she's going to be here soon."

"How could you do that?" Hunter demands. "You know how important it is for us to-"

"I know! I've been kicking myself since it happened! I drove right over here to tell you guys what I did. I know it was wrong. I know it was thoughtless." She glances at Chase. "I'm sorry."

He takes a slow, controlled breath. "Hunter and I have to deal with this meeting. Lief, take our fiancée home and wait for our guests. I'm sure it won't just be Sophia."

I nod once. Hunter's hurt. It's all over his face. He swallows. "Right, I'll bring the guys in."

Valerie's lips part. "We will not talk about-"

"I told you I had ten minutes. If we hadn't spent those ten minutes fucking on this table, we could have talked about it," Chase says. "Go home."

Valerie's face falls, but she doesn't resist when I pull her from the room. She sniffs once and Vasily, the new head of the southern chapter, steps forward. He looks her over and raises an eyebrow at me before speaking in Russian. "Is the girl too good to join us?"

I scoff, but he leans closer as the others laugh. "Is she okay?" I nod once and he inclines his head, then does a double take. "Ah, future Mrs. Volkov."

She nods to him once and answers in Russian as well. "I hope you have a good meeting ..."

"V," he offers her his hand. "Just the letter. My name is uncommon here."

She shakes it. "Because *Lief* is normal."

He chuckles. "Outside of business, I go by my middle name: Lev. Short, easy to remember, fun."

"Nice to meet you," she replies.

"I hope to see you in higher spirits soon. No bride should be so sad. Especially not with three husbands to fix it." He winks at me.

I motion to the doors. "Go ahead in, Vasily. The Volkovs are eager to start."

He nods once, his black hair, scruff on his face, and that scar. Rumor is he got it when he was young, only twenty. An operation went wrong. Since his survival, he doesn't fear god, death, the devil, or anything else. He's made himself into the most dangerous person in every room, despite his easy smile.

I put Valerie in the passenger side of the car and drive us home, looping around to make sure, as always, that we're not being followed. She sniffs again, but I haven't seen a tear, no matter how watery her eyes are.

Not knowing what to say, I say nothing. Valerie groans after twenty minutes. "I know I fucked up! Stop giving me the silent treatment."

"It's rather blue today," I comment, glancing at the sky. "No clouds."

She nods once. "The pollen count is high today. It's bothering allergies in the clinic."

"You told her," I say, addressing the problem.

"I've been so good, never sharing with a soul, and then it just slipped out while I was asking Sophia who she decided to marry on paper," she whispers. "That's all it was supposed to be, but it was so easy for her and I needed to get out my confusion and it just ... it slipped."

Nodding feels right. Within the mafia, we're taught the price of letting our tongue be so free. I saw it when I first joined. Mr. Volkov cut a man's tongue for saying 'mafia' instead of 'business'.

Hunter and Chase had to monitor themselves their whole lives and with examples being made left and right (maiming and death), it was a lesson that became as vital as breathing.

"I understand," I answer, taking her hand. "You haven't been through what we have."

"I know better! I do. It's been clear since I found out. I mean, look what happened to me just by being in the wrong place at the wrong time, then I go and ... fuck," she says. "And then, my stupid ass said, "they're going to kill me" right after that."

I chuckle.

She glowers at me. "It's not funny. We know that's not the case, but Sophia just learned that Chase is the mafia boss. Imagine if you were in my place and you told your best friend that secret, then followed it with 'they'll kill me'. It's like a threat."

"We'll defuse it when they get here. Holden's known about us for a while. He's a hard one to limit when it comes to computers and Chase underestimated him," I say, assuring her.

It doesn't help. I know that the second she goes to the kitchen. She cooks when nervous—and the banging of pots and pans grates on my nerves until I join her.

I prepare a pan and take the potatoes she gives me, so it will be a productive use of time. I season them, mash them once, then stick them in the oven with butter. She's working on a pork rump, but I see her hands shaking.

"Chase and Hunter aren't going to forgive me like you," she murmurs.

"They'll come around," I say, guiding her hands and making it easier. "I heard from the florist. We have a few options to go with. He wants to meet with you to discuss your bouquet."

"You're assuming Hunt and Chase will still want to marry me," Valerie grumbles.

"Doesn't matter to me if they back out. I'm not," I say against her ear. "And you know they can't stay mad at you for long."

She softens against me and nods. "I'm worrying too much."

"The right amount based on our lives," I disagree, kissing her cheek.

We get a meal started and finished by the time rapid fire knocking echoes from the front door. Valerie looks up at me. I have on a pink apron she bought that says, "Forget dessert, taste the chef" and my hair back in a braid.

"I love you, Viking. Always. You know that, right?" she asks.

I nod and kiss her. "At least half as much as I love you, Viper."

She kisses me again, then goes to the door. "Stop banging! I hear you!"

Sophia runs in, followed by the guys. I know Holden didn't share with them, but they're not as worried as Sophia is. Valerie looks between them, being as calm as possible. "You didn't bring Link."

"No, I didn't bring my baby!" Sophia yells. "After what you told me, I'm getting you out of here. Take off the rings and let's-"

Valerie backs up to me. "No."

"This is dangerous! It's wrong. I never should have let the guys introduce you to them," she argues. "If Holden would have told me."

Holden doesn't flinch, he just shrugs. "Didn't tell anyone."

"Then you did better than I did," Valerie grumbles.

I walk behind her and wrap my arms around her. "Should we have Sophia help us pick centerpieces?"

"I'd like that," Valerie agrees, kissing my cheek.

"I need that apron," Gunner says.

"You don't cook," Roman argues. "I like my apron well enough."

"Well, maybe I would cook if I could use it to flirt with-"

"Enough!" Sophia grabs at her hair, then takes both of Valerie's hands. "Why are you with these three? If you just found out, you should be running. You can always come to us and we can set you up in Italy or in ... somewhere safe!"

I stay quiet even as I listen in. I pull up one of the cameras and notice Valerie touching her belly. She looks queasy, upset. She hides anxiety and panic well.

Sophia stares at her hand, and then her eyes bulge. "Oh god, are you pregnant?"

"No!" Valerie yells, before lowering her voice and sucking her bottom lip. "I'm not pregnant. I'm stressed as hell."

"Then why are you doing this ... unless.." Sophia goes quiet, but Valerie doesn't fill in any blanks. She just watches her best friend process, as if Valerie already knows what pieces she's adding together until Sophia stumbles back a step. "You've known about this, haven't you? And that thing at the clinic, that wasn't ... it wasn't some disturbed patient, was it? It was one of *their* enemies trying to kill you."

"Sophia, I need you to take a breath and sit down," Valerie says. "I can see you're about to burst."

"Because my best friend has been throwing herself in danger! My best friend has been lying to me for ... a year! At least! And I'm the reason you had to do it!" She sinks to the couch and her husbands take up the space next to her. Holden places Sophia on his lap and whispers to her.

Valerie looks around and I make my return, still trying to steer the focus away from this problem. If I can get us focused on something else, maybe that will buy me time to minimize the details of our ... adventures. "So, we have ten options."

"Forget the flowers!" Sophia yells. "How long

have you known Valerie? And what the hell have you gotten into?"

Valerie and I share a long look before I nod. I pull her onto my lap, sitting with her in the recliner. The pictures remain in a manilla folder on her knees, an option for her to bring up.

I take a slow breath. "About a month after we all met up at the gala where Valerie came with Gunner, she discovered what we do in the worst way possible. She witnessed me ... following an order."

"That long?! What the hell?" Sophia glowers at Valerie as if I'm not the one talking right now.

"Alright, now we're going to talk about this," Chase booms. "You let it *slip*? That's not something that 'slips', Valerie."

"How did it even come up?" Hunter yells in Russian. "It couldn't have been naturally and-"

"Don't you yell at my best friend!" Sophia orders. "Not when I'm doing the yelling!"

What a headache.

SIX

Valerie

THIS IS TOO MUCH TO HANDLE. HUNTER AND CHASE glower at Sophia. Hunter's the one who gets words out. "How did you get her to spill?"

"She was telling me how she couldn't choose who to marry on paper and it just happened to come up that Chase here is a fucking mafia boss!" Sophia yells. "And that's not the point. The point, Valerie, is that you lied to me."

"They are a business!" I argue. "Anytime they got hurt, I said it was on business and that was true. I did get hurt at work. The man was technically a patient."

"So now you're going technical on me?" she asks.

I rub my arm and Lief kisses my shoulder. He clears his throat and everyone stops talking. Sophia shrinks back. Lief rubs my knee. "We can't have everyone knowing what we do. Of course, Valerie had to keep it a secret, to protect us, to protect you, to protect herself. The more people that know, the more potential danger those people are in. She was doing us all a favor by being lonely and keeping this to herself."

Sophia sucks her bottom lip and tears fill her eyes. "Valerie, how could you do something so dangerous? This isn't skydiving or bungee jumping or anything else we talked about."

"Believe me, I know," I whisper.

Chase shakes his head and walks upstairs, stopping halfway. "For the record, I don't like this conversation at all."

"Too bad we don't have the Men in Black mind eraser," Hunter snorts before going to the kitchen. "These are going to burn."

He takes everything out of the oven and Sophia shakes her head again. "What are you doing?"

"Well, after the first kidnapping, everything seemed easy," I try to joke.

Hunter shakes his head once. I swallow. "Not everything. But the kidnapping was easy compared to seeing my men hurt, thinking about losing them, trying to stay away from them when I loved them. Logic doesn't have a place in love, Sophia. You showed me that."

"Don't you turn this around on me," she hisses. "I married four good men, good *business* men. Sure, they're older and it's not conventional, but I was never in danger!"

"Valerie's the danger," Hunter says, staring at the food. "Talking her way out of death twice. Mocking someone ready to kill her just to buy time and keep me alive. Trying to throw herself into everything so we're not hurt, then facing down a half-crazed ex member just to disarm him, break his arm, and declare herself queen."

There's pride in his voice, even if he won't look at me. Lief nods and squeezes me tighter. "A viper, strong and smart. Refuses to be locked away in a safe room without lashing out when I come back for her."

"Do that again and I will cut you," I say.

Lief kisses me, not caring who's watching. When he draws back, I smile at him. Hunter takes a slow breath. "Valerie came into our life and we hid everything from her until she saw the wrong thing. She wanted to leave us; we knew she needed protection."

"Yeah, the safe house had nothing to do with it," I grumble. Shaking my head, I refocus on Sophia. "If my men had their way, I'd never touch the mafia business. I'd never go to the mansion. I wouldn't be involved in the business at all. Sometimes they need me to psychoanalyze from a distance or up close, but I insist on being there as often as possible."

"Why?" Sophia asks.

"Because I love them. If you could stand by letting your men do everything for you—*everything*—

knowing they were risking their lives, knowing that if you were there, you could help, you could change the odds, could you just stay home?" I ask.

She looks at her men and shakes her head. "No. I couldn't."

"You stayed with them through every argument, through every bit of stress, even when you knew it was a risk to your relationship with your dad, when you knew people wouldn't understand, when you weren't sure how it could work," I remind her. "I'm doing the same thing. I love them, Sophie. I love them enough to propose to them and you know how I've always felt about marriage."

She nods once.

"I wouldn't give up a single terrible moment, a single injury I've endured if it meant losing them. I don't have any doubts about being with them. They're wonderful to me, they're good for me, and we bring out the best in each other," I insist.

"You're overselling, Dorogaya," Hunter says. "We only make you more lethal."

"You make me strong enough to face my father, to deal with my mother, and support me so much I feel like I could run for president, so don't you dare minimize. I'll have to talk to you and Chase about that in counseling," I say.

Hunter takes a slow breath and nods.

Sophia shakes her head. "And Holden, you knew the whole time?"

"I did, but what was the point of saying

anything? It won't change what they were born into or that Valerie loves them, baby." He shrugs.

I can see she's worried about something. She touches her stomach and I perk. "Are *you* pregnant?"

She nods. "Yes. And now I'm wondering how the hell I made you godmother when you're involved in the mafia."

"Because you know that I'd protect your kids with my life and so would my fiancés. In fact, we're more equipped to do that than anyone," I growl.

Roman smirks. "That's an excellent point."

"Aren't mafia's pretty ... traditional?" Gunner asks. "I mean, it was passed down to Chase, bypassing Hunter, but you being involved with three guys in the mafia, you being ... your normal prickly self, how is that working?"

"My father gave her a gun for an engagement present," Hunter informs us while sipping from some vodka. "Brandy, Gunner?"

"Please," he groans.

Chase comes downstairs. He takes a slow breath. "I'm not happy with you, Valerie. You violated our trust."

"I know," I whisper.

"But I understand that you're stressed and you're used to telling Sophia everything, since I know you told her about plenty in our relationship. It's a good thing you held back for as long as you did," Chase says.

"Do you still love me?" I ask in Russian.

His face falls, and he crosses the space between us to kiss me. "I never stopped, baby doll. I can be mad and love you at the same time. I've figured that out."

I nod once and squeeze his hand.

Sophia looks between us and takes a slow breath. "I'm still going to worry about you."

"I know," I say with a smile. "Because you're an amazing best friend."

"I'm the *best* best friend," she says, sighing. "And that means knowing I'm not going to pry you from them and admitting ... that I've never seen anyone make you so happy. Even when you were hooking up with that drummer who ended up being famous."

"Who?" Hunter demands. "He can become *un*famous fast."

"I'll tell you when you give me a list of your conquests, Krolik," I dare.

He swallows more vodka? Sophia pats her legs. "Okay. Let's see the floral arrangements."

Lief, Sophie and I go over the options. I can see how much Lief likes the purple orchids and the white ones that are splattered with purple alongside the baby's breath and the gold-painted carnations.

"I think this one will work the best," Sophia points at the blue and white orchids with the lavender and yellow roses. "It's romantic, but not over the top. People will still be able to see each other, and you won't have petals everywhere."

"I like the lilies," Chase fills in as he rejoins us. "I think yellow and purple work well together.

I nod in agreement. "But I do like the gold carnations, considering the venue."

Lief kisses my temple. "I'm glad you noticed they tie in."

"Your father gave you some décor mastery," I tease.

"You have a venue!" Sophia bounces. "Show me!"

I show her the pictures from the website and the ones I took. She coos over it. We talk all about how we're going to do dresses—I want even her in bright colors—and all the things she wished she would have known while planning.

"When's the date?" Roman asks.

"Two and a half months," Hunter answers. "A shame it couldn't be half that."

"You might still be mad at me," I say.

He shakes his head with a wicked smile. I narrow my eyes. "What did you find?"

"I happened to find a Christmas present in my office last night. It's something you should wear," he hints.

Ah, the sexy librarian costume. I flush anyway and nod. "I know you."

"Very well," he agrees.

"Okay, well then we have to go wedding dress

shopping next week. Come up to the city, there are so many other options, plus your men won't see it," Sophia insists.

"We're buying it," Lief argues.

"Like hell you are," Sophia and I say together.

We laugh, have dinner, and things get easier. It feels good. I like not having to hide things from Sophia. I show her the pretty knife Lief got me and she rolls her eyes. Chase excuses himself, still not happy with the situation or me, but overall, everything feels good.

Sophia sighs. "I'm tempted to ask to stay, but I have a feeling you guys make up as violently as you live."

"You'd be correct." Hunter raises his glass to her. "You're as quick as Valerie is."

"And I have a feeling your husbands want to make the most of having a babysitter right now." I wiggle my eyebrows at Gunner.

He shoots me finger guns. "You get me."

"Yeah, yeah. You guys get out of here. I'll try to come up to New York this weekend so I don't have to take off more work than necessary," I say, promising.

"We're still going to talk about you working on one of those online platforms," Lief says.

"Agreed," Sophia chirps. "Keep her away from the dangers of the public."

"Hey!" I butt in. "I enjoy helping people."

"You can do it online," Sophia says before

kissing my cheek and hugging me. "Stay sane until we see each other in New York?"

"I'll bring some guests," I say, as I squeeze her.

"Good. And call Danny. She's waiting to hear from you. She doesn't know about all this." Sophia motions to Hunter and Lief. "And if Chase raises his voice at you, I'll send Nick over. You should hear his dad voice."

Nick stands a little taller and winks at Sophia. "You like it far too much."

I slump on the couch when they leave. Hunter walks over to me and offers me a shot of flavored vodka. I throw it back and sigh. "It's been a long day. How was the meeting?"

Hunter shrugs. "I couldn't focus on it. I was thinking of you crying, feeling guilty. In all honesty, I slipped once. How do you think Lief got brought in?"

Lief waves at me. "I told my mom."

"You what?" Hunter jerks around to face him.

"She asked what was new. I told her I joined the mafia because it had wonderful benefits and I could take care of my anger issues. She supported me," he explained.

"I've been tiptoeing around it with your family!" Hunter argues.

"Chase slipped too," Lief informs.

Hunter and I stare at him. He rubs his chin. "He was drunk. It was right after they put me on security. Drunk, flirting, and the girl didn't believe him at all. I don't know if she even heard him. Sometimes, we need to tell something big, even if no one hears it."

"I love you," I say to both of them. "That's something I need you both to hear more often."

SEVEN

Hunter

"THIS IS WHAT WE NEED TO MAKE UP?" VALERIE asks.

I rest my feet on my desk while adjusting the book in my lap. I haven't read a single page. A few minutes after Sophia left, Chase and Lief left to take care of something at the mansion, leaving Valerie and me alone.

"With me, I think it is," I answer.

She sighs. "This is supposed to be used when you're happy."

She should know I've already forgiven her. This is all for fun, which is what we need. Plus, Chase got pre-fight sex and Lief got to have her back with Sophia, so I deserve to have her all to myself.

"Are you coming out or are you going to keep hiding, Dorogaya?" I ask.

She sighs and walks into the room. She has on a see-through button up tied just under her breasts, a little red tie, and a miniskirt that's tight around her thighs and keeps trying to pull up to her waist. She adjusts the thigh highs and then looks up at me. Valerie's dark hair is back in a twist and she has on some fake glasses, too. Of course, she wore some sexy red lipstick because she knows how it riles me up.

I cock my head to the side and rub over my jaw. I'd turn in every book on time, I'd spend every single day at the library, making a mess, if Valerie was dressed up like this catering to me.

"That book is past due," she says, pointing at the book that just so happens to be covering my raging hard on. "I'll need it back with the late fee."

"But I haven't finished it yet."

She narrows her eyes at me and walks closer. I see her hand itching towards the hem of her skirt, but she doesn't pull it down. Instead, she pushes my feet off the desk and points at me as her glasses slide down her nose. "Hunter Volkov, you will pay the fee, no matter what. You not finishing the book isn't my fault. Play by the rules."

I smirk. "I don't like rules."

"Isn't that a shame?" She steps closer. "I like good boys who follow the rules."

She reaches for the book, but I hold it in place, arching an eyebrow. "Are you going to steal a book from me?"

Valerie glares back. "Hunter, you will pay for the pleasure of reading this book."

"I'm more than happy to do so. The problem is, I don't have any cash on me."

"Then you'd better find another way to pay."

"You mentioned pleasure. Maybe I'm not the only one who should have some pleasure." I put the book on the desk and pull Valerie onto my lap. She gasps and braces herself against me as some of her hair slips free of her clip. I smirk. "I could pay you that way."

"That sounds like you getting what you want and a book," she says.

"Not if I focus on your pleasure alone," I say, as I set her on the desk. "I have to pay you. I can do that with my fingers or my mouth and then I get nothing out of it."

"Uh-huh," she says, not buying it.

"The late fee would be three dollars. I'll give you three orgasms instead," I barter.

Valerie's lips part, and she takes a ragged breath. "Three?"

I set her on the desk and lean over her. I brush my lips across her, press my mouth to the corner of hers, then continue kissing until I suck her earlobe. She shudders and I hear her nails scrape against the wood.

"First, I'll get you in the mood, licking and sucking your hard nipplcs, thcn I'll slide my hand between your soft thighs and rub your clit until you're soaking wet for me," I purr in her ear.

She pants. I pull her hips closer to me, so she

has to spread her legs. Her skirt leaps up around her waist, revealing crotchless red panties. I nibble at her throat. "Once you're wet, I'll sink my fingers into you, fingering you until you come apart for me."

"Hunt," she whimpers. I don't know if I've ever talked dirty to her without touching her.

"You don't like that arrangement? I haven't even gotten to the best part," I tease, sucking the hollow under her ear and grinding against her. "Don't you want to know what I have in mind?"

"Yes, but just ... just to see if it will cover what you owe," she says.

I grin and bite her throat. "Once you come for my fingers, I'll spread your legs around my shoulders and devour you, taking my time so you get to enjoy it. While I eat your pussy, you can taste yourself on my fingers. That'll make sure neither of us is too loud when you come for me."

"You sound confident that you'll make me come ... what if you don't?" she asks.

I laugh. "We both know that's not a problem. I'll make you come with my tongue, then I'll fuck you. I'll give you everything you need, pounding into you right on this desk. Even if I don't come, you will. Then I can keep my book."

"Well, that ... that could work." Valerie trembles.

I grin and kiss her hard. She melts against me, her hands tugging at my shirt, pulling at me as I grip her hips tight and feast on her mouth. Her tongue curls with mine and my erection rubs against my pants.

"Is that a yes? Will it fulfill what I owe?" I ask against her mouth.

"That depends on how well you follow through on your plan," she answers.

Grinning, I undo her shirt and cup her breast in my hand. I circle her nipple with my thumb, then tug it. Her lips part and she squirms. "Hunt.."

Guiding her back further, I wrap my lips around her hard nipple, sucking and licking, teasing her with little flicks of my tongue as my fingers slide up her thigh and press against her clit. I circle my fingers, taking my time even though she's soaking wet. She bucks against my hand.

I keep teasing her with light touches, taking my time, enjoying the way she writhes for more. I switch to her other nipple, flatting my tongue over it before sucking hard and massaging with my teeth. She groans and wraps one hand around the back of my head.

"I'm so wet," Valerie says.

Taking that cue, I slide my fingers into her tight pussy. She moans and digs her nails into the back of my neck as she rolls her hips against my hand. I slide a third finger into her. I tap her g-spot, then curl my fingers inside her.

I exploit every spot she likes as she whines and whimpers. I suck her nipple hard and she comes for me. Her pussy tightens around my fingers, gripping me tight like she can't get enough.

"Yes, Krolik, you are so good. Feel ... so good," she moans as she comes, soaking my fingers.

I kiss and lick up her breast, along her throat, and claim her mouth again as I keep thrusting my fingers into her, in and out on repeat, until her orgasm ebbs. I draw back and she shudders, trying to squeeze her legs together.

"There's one. Do you remember the next part?" I ask.

She nods.

I sink to my knees and spread her legs over my shoulders, jerking her closer to the edge until her pussy is right in my face. I lick over her slit and her thighs tighten. I hold her ass in my hands as I lick her up and down, from entrance to clit, focusing more and more on her clit until Valerie whimpers. I offer her my wet fingers as I lift my eyes to her flushed face.

She sucks them, but I thrust further in her mouth as I suck her clit and tongue her. I try to take my time, I do. I want Valerie to enjoy this, want her to know how much she means to me. But her tongue stroking between my fingers, the soft sucking sounds and her muffled moans spur me on.

I groan and devour her pussy, sucking, licking, kissing everything she loves until I set a pace that has her legs tightening around me, trying to drag me closer. She squeezes my head between her thighs and bites my fingers as she comes. I love how she tenses and trembles for me.

Standing up, I free my fingers from her mouth. Her lips are shiny with her own wetness and her eyes are all glassy.

"Were you worried you weren't going to come?" I ask.

She shakes her head and pulls me against her, kissing me like she needs. Valerie pushes me back onto the chair and mounts me, as her hands are busy with my pants. "I want you."

"Do you? I thought I was paying a fine," I tease.

"Fuck the fine," she growls as she jerks my pants down. "I want your cock buried deep inside me *now.*"

I thrust into her, and we moan together. Valerie rides me with blatant determination. She kisses me deep, pulls my hair, scratches at my shirt and rubs herself on me until we fall backwards. She moans, but doesn't stop, continuing to take me like she needs me.

I roll her over and hold her down. "I'm going to make you come, over and over again."

"Yes," she gasps. "Until you finish, Krolik. Don't stop."

I give her everything she wants, plowing into her over and over again, fucking her through her third orgasm as I grip her thigh over my hip, then put her legs over my shoulders. I kiss her as her hips lift to take every inch of my thick cock.

"Hunter! I can't ... I ... too much, too-"

She comes again, gushing over my cock as her pussy tries to pull me deeper inside her. I wrap my hand around her throat and kiss her parted lips just before my stomach tightens and ecstasy sweeps through me. I come with her.

My heart pounds in my ears, louder than any sound Valerie or I make until I collapse on top of her. She shudders and strokes my back. "You can keep the book."

"I'd rather keep you," I answer.

She giggles and runs her fingers through my hair. "Are you still angry with me?"

"No." I sigh. "I'm very pleased right now."

She lifts my chin and kisses me. "You know Sophia won't say anything. Holden won't let her and she wouldn't hurt me ... or us."

I nod. "I know."

"Valerie? Hunter?" Chase calls from downstairs.

I grin at her and kiss her again. "I hope you're ready for the rest of the makeup sex you're about to get."

"I should get out of this costume," she murmurs, despite not making a move to get up.

I grab her wrists and hold her down. "I don't remember saying I was done with you."

She moans and kisses me. A few minutes later, Lief and Chase join in. Chase doesn't ask a single question. He just gets on his knees as I flip Valerie onto all fours. She takes him in her mouth as I fuck her again. Lief strokes himself as he watches. Who needs therapy or communication when we can just take care of every fight or frustration like this?

By the time all of us finish, Valerie lies between Lief and Chase, only half awake. Chase cups her chin. "I'm sorry for my reaction."

"I'm sorry for outing you," she answers against his lips.

Just like that, all is right in the world.

EIGHT

Valerie

I KISS EACH OF MY FIANCÉS AS I GET ON THE PLANE. Lief holds me in place for an extra moment. "I don't like you flying alone."

"Is a ghost going to get me in the sky, Lief?" I tease. "The pilot will take good care of me."

"If he doesn't, let us know," Chase says just loud enough for the flight staff to hear. I know no one will cross him.

"And let us know when you arrive," Hunter insists.

"Guys, I'm going to be gone for a day and a half," I say, kissing each of them again. "I'm more worried about you three getting into trouble and me not being around to save your very nice asses."

"We'll keep our asses safe," Chase promises.

"Yeah, you better," I poke his chest. "Boss or not, you know I'll be angry."

Hunter puts Chase in a headlock. "I have a lifetime of practice keeping him in line."

Lief rolls his eyes. "I promise, everything will be fine. No threats have come in."

"We could always come with you," Chase says after shoving Hunter to the side.

Instead, a car pulls up. Vanya and Josefine get out with Elaine, all giggling. I motion to them. "The plane is full."

The guys pout, but we have an amazing plane ride. We drink champagne, I flip through bridal magazines and point out dresses I like. I show Elaine some bridesmaid gowns and we're all a little tipsy when we land. Rather than burdening Sophie with housing so many people, we get a hotel and continue the fun, ordering room service and talking about nothing.

When Vanya and Josefine decide to go out to enjoy New York, I sigh as I lie out on the bed next to Elaine.

"I can't believe you're getting married to three guys. Like I knew because of the Halloween party you were seeing all three of them, but I just assumed it was a fling, you know?" she asks. "Then we graduate and bam, you're engaged."

I laugh. "I know. It all happened kind of fast, but I love them. I'd do ..." I think about the things I have done for my fiancés. "I do anything for them. I don't want to wait to be their wife."

"So ..." she rolls onto her belly and draws circles

on the comforter. "Who are you marrying? I know you want all three, but legally speaking."

"I'm thinking about marrying Lief. I'm worried if I marry Chase or Hunter, they'll be jealous. Not the best way to start a marriage," I mumble.

"Agreed."

"So it just seems better that way, but there are complications, so I don't know. Oddly, they haven't talked to me about it. I think they're just assuming I'll end up with the Volkov name."

"I mean, the odds are in the favor of that," Elaine hints. "Two out of three, you know?"

I smirk and pass her another drink. "They should know better than to assume."

We giggle and tease each other until we fall asleep. The next morning, Sophia picks us all up in a limo. She beams and offers us champagne while she drinks water. We talk about dresses and go back and forth about ideas. Josefine would love to see me in a ball gown looking like a princess. Vanya can't picture me in white. Elaine says a mermaid would highlight my figure the best, and Sophia just keeps watching my face with a grin.

"Be drop dead sexy, like your normal self," she says when everyone else is silent. "By the way, Danny is meeting us there."

"Great," I say with a smile before downing the rest of my glass.

Danny joins us at the dress shop. Sophia promised that this was the place with the best selection and the most varied dresses. Some are one of a kind, others are so exclusive they might as well be one of a kind.

The attendant brings us more alcohol–apparently it's a huge part of dress shopping–and we all sit on two plush couches. Danny squeezes my hand. "I can't believe you're going to be in a wedding dress."

"I know," I breathe.

"Try on a princess gown, something fit for a queen," Vanya says with a wink.

"And something fitting," Elaine insists. "Something that's you."

The opinion's fly. The attendant looks at me. "Something unique. And a second dress, something shorter, for the reception."

All eyes go to me for that. Sophia didn't have to worry about that. I doubt Danny did either, but Vanya nods. "A good plan."

"The budget?" the attendant asks.

I open my mouth to give one, but Josefine puts a hand on my knee. "There isn't one."

I roll my eyes, but soon enough, I'm in a huge poofy gown. I like the top, the sweetheart style that hints at sex appeal, but doesn't make it the focus. I like that it has a corset, but after two steps, I hate the weight of the dress and the tulle fabric rubbing against me.

After Sophia sees my face, she shakes her head. "Next!"

Did they bring snacks? I glower at her, and she winks while popping another little pastry in her mouth. Danny winks at me. "We have to stay entertained, too."

After three dresses that I just don't mesh with and refuse to come out in, I'm exhausted. The attendant brings me something very different. It's all lace with some kind of fabric under it that matches my skin tone but keeps me from showing everything off. She clamps me into it and I look at the way it flows over my body.

"That's the best face I've seen so far," she comments.

"I like how fitted it is. I'm not sure about all this patterning though," I admit before shrugging and walking out.

Elaine and Danny both cock their heads to the side as I stand in front of the mirror and look myself over again. It's pretty, but I don't think it's me. I turn around and Vanya sighs. "It's beautiful."

Sophia gives it a thumbs down. "The fit yes, the style, no."

"Yeah," Danny agrees. "You just don't look like you in it."

Josefine taps her bottom lip, then gets up. I groan. "If you guys are getting more snacks, I'm going to murder you."

"Okay, so less décor. How do you feel about shimmer or bling?" the attendant asks as I strip again and sip from my champagne. Now I under-stand the appeal of alcohol.

"Not great. I just want to feel ..." I try to find the word. "Elegantly beautiful, but not soft or anything like that. I'm sorry I'm so picky. I'm sure I'm not making your job easy."

"I'd rather you be honest than try to please me. It's your day and you should look forward to every bit of it," she says. "I'm going to check for some additional fitted dresses like this with less detailing and more of that oomph to them."

"Thank you," I say with a little sigh.

My phone buzzes and I see it's Chase. I answer and wait for him to speak. "Are you in a mood already, baby doll?"

"Trying on dresses is a workout," I complain.

He chuckles. "We can always wear pajamas instead."

"Absolutely not!" Hunter yells from the background.

I roll my eyes and smile. "Maybe just a silk robe for me, then?"

"Don't tease," Chase groans.

"I don't know if I'll come back with a dress. I know I'll figure it out before the wedding and it's nice to get time with everyone," I murmur. "Are all of you okay? Good ... uninjured."

"Yes, baby doll. It's just been meetings. One man is close to taking over in the south."

"The Lev guy I met?" I ask.

"That's the one," Chase pauses. "When did you meet him?"

"It was the world's shortest conversation. I hear the attendant coming back. Love you three," I bid before hanging up.

She comes back with three more dresses. One has gold filigree on the bottom and I think I'll like it until I put it on and see the way the fabric changes for the mermaid part of the skirt at the end. I shake my head.

Just as I'm about to say a real 'fuck no' to the third one, there's a knock on the door. I slump back and Josefine peeks in with a dress. "Try this one."

"Really?" the attendant asks.

"I saw it when we walked in and I think she'll love it. Sophie already agreed and so did Elaine," Josefine says to me.

I perk up. Sophie and Elaine have opposite tastes. I wiggle into the gown and stare at myself in the mirror. I turn around to look at the lace detailing on the back and beam.

"There we go. A smile," the attendant puts a hand to her chest. "I didn't think it was possible."

I walk out and look at myself in all three mirrors. I don't like the sleeves draping over my arms, but I like the cut, the hint at cleavage without showing any, the way it fits to my body until the knees where the white fabric spreads like a trumpet. Not to mention the lace trail that acts like a halo along the bottom of the dress, even if longer in the back. The little side cuts that reveal lace and my skin, stopping just at my hips as if it's tracing my body is perfect.

"The back is amazing. The way the lace covers until your butt," Sophia hums.

"Plus, it shows so much of your back!" Elaine claps. "Valerie, you're gorgeous."

"Can I take off these sleeves?" I ask.

The attendant removes them. The dress looks even better. I feel confident, powerful, but beautiful and regal at the same time. My eyes water as I imagine my men seeing me. Turning around, I face my audience.

Danny smiles, then bites her lip. "That dress was made for you, Valerie."

"It's a perfect fit for you and your personality," Vanya whispers, dabbing at her eyes.

I laugh once and cover my mouth. I thought getting emotional over a dress was just a T.V. thing. I sniff and then the attendant brings over a veil with the same lace details. She puts it on and shows it to me.

"This is the one," I whisper. "It is."

I can't believe I found it. After looking online and being disappointed, not wanting to try a single thing on, to going through a mountain of dresses, I have the one I want. I'm stuck in a group hug, then freed as we look at shorter dresses for the reception. I find a nice high-low dress I can hide a knife under since that's mandatory for our reception, and can dance in. It even looks like it's meant to pair with my gown.

"Okay, now you guys get to try on bridesmaids' dresses while I drink and eat. Let's go," I order.

Danny, Elaine, and Sophia all groan, but obey. I pop little cookies into my mouth while drinking water and watch them try on plenty of gowns until we select a color and style that works for all three of them.

Nick comes in a few minutes later, his eyes covered. "Am I allowed to look?"

"Hi, Nick," I say. "Your wife is changing back into her normal clothes. Join us."

"Did you get a dress?" he asks.

"I got two," I answer.

"Good, then the celebration dinner will have a reason," he says with a bright smile.

Before I can pay for my dress, Vanya and Josefine split it, saying they never got to do it for a daughter, then we're off to dinner, laughing and enjoying the best New York offers, including the best company I could ask for.

NINE

Chase

"OKAY," I SAY WITH A SIGH AS I LOOK AT THE wedding list with Hunter, Lief, and our fathers. "We got our tuxes, we have the venue. We have the caterer, the florist, the photographer, and the cake. We've got the list of people to invite, so I think we just need to send out the invitations, write our vows, settle on security locations, and find an officiant."

"Plenty to do in just over two months," my father says.

"Not too much," Hunter argues. "How hard can invitations be?"

"There's also the seating arrangement, choosing the first dance song, the other major dances, like Valerie with her father, you three with your mothers, who's walking who down the aisle, if you're doing flower girls, whether you're inviting children," Roger points out.

I share a look with Hunter and Lief. Lief

handles this one. "Valerie's parents aren't invited to the ceremony. We invited her mother to the reception. I believe Tristan will walk her down the aisle."

"Her parents," Father huffs.

I narrow my eyes at him, and he holds his hands up. "We can figure out everything on the list. There's only one question I have."

"What?" Hunt asks.

"Why hasn't Valerie asked Chase to go with her to get a marriage license?"

The room stays quiet. I've never assumed Valerie was going to choose to marry me on paper. I'd like it. I know that. Each of us would. However, I have a feeling she's still deciding, considering she was talking to Sophia about it.

Roger nods. "She hasn't decided who's she's marrying."

"It's obvious. She has to marry you, Chase. You're the boss," father argues.

"Right, because marrying second best would be terrible," Hunter growls.

"I'm not saying that it would be bad for you and her to get married. I'm stating that she should have the Volkov name so all know she's with Chase," he explains.

"I doubt she wants to be Dr. Volkov at work. Imagine the attention it would draw," Lief murmurs.

"Oh, so her last name should be Prins?" Hunter demands.

"A strong last name," Roger agrees.

"Or she can keep her own," I point out.

All eyes go to me. I put my hands up. "I'm saying that she isn't obligated to take our last name. She can be whoever she wants."

"This is a conversation that needs to happen soon. You'll want to get that process started," Father says.

I check the time. "Valerie will be at the airport soon. We should go."

We head to the airport, and the car is silent. We've managed to double check a great deal and to narrow down the list of the ceremony and the reception. Father wanted us to invite only business associates, but we nixed that. We'll invite the heads of each house, then family and friends. Father insisted on security and so we've chosen our security guards. Everything is taken care of…mostly.

Valerie steps off the plane, looking gorgeous as she clings to Elaine. She kisses Elaine's cheek and sends her off with Vanya and Josefine. Both mothers wave to us.

Hunter sweeps Valerie up in his arms and kisses her. "Did you get a dress?"

"Yes, they're doing some alterations, so it will fit me. I can't gain any weight before the big day now," she says, laughing.

Lief hugs her and kisses the top of her head. "I don't like not coming home to you. It defeats the purpose of being retired."

"Half retired," she corrects Lief.

I wrap my arms around Valerie and breathe her in. I don't enjoy being without her. I don't want her in another house, let alone another state. I kiss the top of her head, between her eyebrows, then her mouth. I suck her bottom lip and draw out every curl of my tongue until she moans against my lips.

"Baby doll, are you happy with your dress?"

"I'm happy with both of them," she assures me. "Have any issues come up?"

"One," Hunter says.

Lief doesn't like it, I can tell. Hunter shakes his head. "It can wait. Let's get home and get you fed."

We do just that, taking her home and putting food in her belly. She tells us about trying on dresses and how exhausted she was doing it, but how much fun she had with everyone. We listen with rapt attention when she says Vanya forced her into a huge skirt that she couldn't stand.

"You dressed like a princess in some giant skirt is something I'd pay to see," Hunter teases.

"I could have hidden a sword and an entire armory under it," she scoffs. "Viking, you would have fit under there with no one noticing."

"I take it back. I wish you would have gotten it," he says with a naughty smile.

"Oh yeah, because you three could tolerate being a whole foot away from me thanks to fabric," she snorts.

I grin. "Absolutely not. That skirt would have been ripped."

Once she finishes eating, Valerie sits back and looks between the three of us. "I'm missing something."

"We narrowed down the invite list and decided on security. All we have to do is send invites, do the seating chart, find an officiant, write our vows, and set up the marriage license," I say.

Hunter nods. "Which has raised more than one question."

Valerie's face pales. "You three ... You know I love you all."

"That doesn't answer who you're marrying on paper or if you're changing your last name, Dr. Sex," Hunter says.

"It's expected for me to marry Chase, isn't it?" She looks at us when we say nothing. She shrinks between her shoulders. "It's not a choice, is it, baby boy?"

"I don't care what my father or the rest of the mafia expects. We can keep secret who you marry on paper and you can choose whatever last name you want. You can keep your own last name. All of us are okay with that," I assure her.

Hunter and Lief nod.

"It's only a piece of paper. I know I'll be married to you either way." Hunter reaches for Valerie's hand.

She takes it. "Thank you, Krolik. I don't want

anyone jealous or upset. We should only be happy on our wedding day."

"Throw a real curve ball and refuse to marry any of us on paper," Lief dares. Hunter and I shoot him glares. He holds up his hand. "It was a joke."

Valerie squeezes Hunter's hand and meets my eyes. "I love you Chase. I know everyone wants me to marry you. I know that. But ... the wife of a Mafia Boss puts me and everyone I love in a lot more danger. Even if it's just on paper, it's public record, Chase."

"I know," I mumble. "I won't be hurt if it's not me."

"If it's not you," she keeps my gaze. "It can't be Hunter either." Her gaze switches to him. "I love you Krolik. I can't wait to call you my husband, but I know what I have to do for me and us. We made our engagement somewhat public and I know that anyone with half a brain knows I'm with you both, but a paper trail ..."

"I understand, Dorogaya. I'm your husband either way ... in all ways. We all are." Hunter takes a slow breath. "And if you're going to marry Lief on paper, I recommend taking his last name."

"Prins," Lief says with pride. "Valerie Prins."

She smiles. "Valerie Prins, it is, as long as everyone is okay with that."

"Yes," Hunter says.

I nod my head. "We all get you, Valerie. That's what matters."

"Agreed. Although, I think we need to spice up our wedding night. Also, there's one thing that's been tragically overlooked. I'm hurt." Hunter pouts.

"What did we forget on our very long list?" Lief asks.

"Other than the songs, as Father pointed out?" I ask.

"The honeymoon!" Hunter yells. "Where are we going? What's the plan? How long can we spare?"

Valerie laughs. She laughs once, then another bubbles out, and another. She shakes her head. "Out of everything?"

"Yes, that's what I'm focused on!" Hunter complains. "I'm tempted to say Mexico again, but we already went there. What if we went to Rio?"

"Rio sounds amazing. My passport is still good," Valerie says.

"Rio's safe ground," I agree. I don't see any issues with that. Our honeymoon should be perfect, lovely, everything we've dreamed about. "Do you care about location, though, Hunter?"

"Just because I'm going to make sure there's no chance of an annulment doesn't mean we don't deserve a gorgeous view," Hunter says, before winking at Valerie.

She rolls her eyes. "Plenty of sex and a view. I'm sure we'll have a good amount to do too."

"Rio will be nice at that time of year. Right

before winter, so it should be lovely," Lief agrees. "Based on the current schedule, we should be able to do two weeks there. We'll have to come back, but ..."

"But living with our wife will be a constant honeymoon," I assure them. "Don't you think so, baby doll?"

"I know so," she bites her bottom lip. "You know, we spent two entire nights apart. We can fix that with a preview of what's in store for the honeymoon, right?"

I grin and I see Hunter and Lief grinning as well. I jump up, throw Valerie over my shoulder, and head to our bedroom. She giggles and swats my ass.

Tossing her on the bed, she wiggles and pulls at her clothing until she's naked in front of us. Hunter grips the footboard. Lief doesn't hesitate. He walks over to Valerie while stripping his shirt and kisses her while grabbing her breast in his big hand. She moans and rolls to give him more of her attention.

I grip her ankle and Hunter grins at me, pulling her other ankle. We tie her to the footboard and she moans.

"We're getting kinky tonight?" Valerie asks.

Lief turns her chin to face him. "Isn't sleeping with three men always kinky?"

"I don't know, sometimes you guys are vanilla," she teases.

I get on her other side and tie her wrist down.

She moans as she's stretched across the bed. I spread her legs, making it easy for Hunter to get on his knees between her thighs and stroke her pussy.

"You're not wet enough to handle us, vanilla or kinky, Dorogaya. Do I need to give you play-by-plays again?" Hunter asks.

She whimpers. "I just want all of you. To fuck me, to love me, then to fall asleep in the same bed as me."

"Oh, is that all?" I ask.

"It's what I'm going to expect on a regular basis, as your wife," Valerie says before stretching to kiss me. "You'd better get used to it, baby boy. Especially since I know how capable you are of pleasing me."

Groaning, I kiss her deeper. Valerie whimpers against my lips and her head falls back. I see Hunter using his fingers and his mouth on her as Lief sucks her nipple and squeezes her free breast, his fingers tightening around her.

"I love seeing you in ecstasy," I say against her parted lips. "This is going to be your forever, baby doll."

TEN

Valerie

THE WEEK PASSES BY. HUNTER, CHASE, LIEF, AND I fall into a routine. Work, rotating who cooks or orders food, and then taking care of wedding plans. Mafia business stays quiet, thankfully, but the reception seating chart is proving to be more difficult. Now that we've got invitations sent out and some RSVPs are coming in, we're hitting the "plus one problem" as Sophia calls it.

I stare at our number of seats available and chew on the tip of my pen. I want people to mingle, but I want them to enjoy themselves too. A part of me wonders if we need a seating chart at all. Can't people just sit where they want?

"You're sexy when you're focused like that," Chase comments, making me jump.

He kisses the top of my head. "You didn't hear me come in?"

"No," I sigh, relaxing into his hands as he rubs

my shoulders. "Do we need a seating chart?"

"We should start with some order. Plus, do you want our mafia friends interacting with your coworkers?" he asks.

"They'll interact, anyway. It's a wedding. I trust that they can keep their mouths shut even with the open bar," I murmur.

Chase kisses my temple, my cheek, then turns my chin to kiss me full on the mouth. "I haven't told you I love you today."

"I love you, baby boy," I sigh. "How was work?"

"Boring. My mother and father were about to head out on a date, so Hunter is ..." Chase's face screws up as he tries to find the word. He shakes his head. "He's frustrated."

"He's not the only one." I push my phone toward Chase. "My mother is very upset with me."

"Is she?"

"For multiple reasons," I grumble.

Chase looks over the texts and shakes his head. "She's upset she wasn't invited to the wedding dress trip?"

"That," I agree, "but she's also demanding that I tell my father about the wedding because she doesn't feel comfortable keeping it from him."

"I thought they weren't talking," he answers.

"They're not supposed to be, but she wants to reconcile with him. She's convinced that he's going to stay on the wagon this time. As if he ever lasts once he has her back." I set the pen down and lean back in the chair, closing my eyes. "If I tell him, he'll want to come. When he finds out he's not allowed, he'll be a problem again."

"We know how to handle problems," Hunter says. "Who's the problem in this case?"

"Our fiancée's father," Chase answers.

"Easy enough to handle," Hunter says with a shrug.

I shoot him a glare. Hunter walks over and wipes at my lip. "Your lip is black."

"The pen," I mumble. "We're not *taking care of* my father. He can wallow in his isolation and misery, knowing his children want nothing to do with him."

"Vicious," Hunter says with obvious approval. He kisses me despite the ink stain on my lips. "Security will keep uninvited guests out. You remember Konstantin, don't you?"

I shake my head.

Hunter rolls his eyes. "The only guy I've ever met who might be bigger than Lief."

"Ah, the one I'm not allowed to look at because you get jealous?" I remember.

Hunter narrows his eyes. "I'm not jealous."

Chase takes my hand and pulls me away from the seating chart to sit on the couch with him. "You sound pretty jealous, Hunt."

"Shut it; I'm not. The point is, he'll keep your father out," Hunter assures. "And your mother if you don't want her there."

"She's allowed to come to the reception, but not the ceremony. She played nice with your moms and she was worried about me after Yuri, but I know she doesn't like I'm marrying you three, that I've been living with you, and everything else," I say.

"Have you talked about it?" Chase asks.

Hunter doesn't argue, and I glower at them both. "You think she's changed just because she met your mothers and I got hurt?"

"You say communication is key," Hunter reminds me. "Maybe you should take her to a counseling session and talk things out ... if you want, of course."

I open my mouth, ready to tell him how pointless that is, but Hunter knows he has me snared. He didn't want to talk to his mother, and I encouraged it. If I say no, that means he doesn't have to keep working on his relationship with her.

As the gears click into place, he smiles. "I'll bribe you."

"No bribes," Chase says while wrapping his arms around me. "Valerie can talk to her mother after the wedding."

"It's up to you. I'm not thrilled about our father and Vanya being at the wedding, but I know they won't object," Hunter sighs.

"We're not having that option in the ceremony," Lief decides as he gets home. He smiles at me. "I refuse to let anyone object."

"Agreed," Chase says.

"It used to be tradition for the best man to have a dagger so he could fend off anyone who would stop the ceremony. We could bring that back," Hunter offers.

I roll my eyes. "No one gets to object because it's our choice. It's that simple."

Lief kisses me. "Viper, are you stressing again?"

"Maybe," I narrow my eyes. "Why?"

"I got a call from the photographer. They aren't available on our wedding date."

"What!" I yell.

He holds his hand out. "There are other photographers. We'll find one."

"Remember when you said the details don't matter," Chase says. "We still have time."

I take a few deep breaths and nod. More problems roll in as the week continues. The venue has renovations. Some of the mafia guests want to add a plus four instead of a plus one, and I'm worried that it's not going to be warm enough for me to be comfortable in either dress by the end of April. I want to pull out my hair and no amount of kisses or cuddling with my fiancés seems to help get my growing worry under control.

"I can feel the tension rolling off of you, Valerie," Lief says. "Stress can lead to more headaches, anxiety, and worse sleep."

"I know, Lief," I snap, before making myself take a breath. "I wouldn't be so stressed if things would just go the way they are supposed to."

"There's time for us to make sure everything happens as it should. It's not just the four of us doing things. My parents are more than willing to set things up. I know Vanya will help if you ask. We have Sophia and her husbands, as well as your brother," Lief says.

I nod once, but say nothing. Lief pulls me into his arms, first hugging me, then rubbing out my neck, down my shoulders, and continuing down my back. "Once we get dinner started, why don't we go spend some time in our sauna? Or you can spar with the punching bag."

"That might be nice," I agree. "Why do I feel like it's easier to deal with Chase and Hunter's enemies than to plan a wedding?"

"Because you tend to have more control in combat, whether it's mental combat or physical," Lief answers.

He presses a kiss on my temple. "Send Hunter to take care of things. He can mix intimidation and charm."

"What about you?" I ask. "You're plenty sexy and charming."

Before Lief answers, the doorbell rings. I look around him to the door and he follows my gaze for a moment, then glances at me. "Are you expecting someone?"

"No," I say. "It could be someone trying to sell something."

Lief pulls out his phone to check security and

his eyes darken. I catch his hand. "Lief?"

"Stay here."

"What? Why?" I ask, still trying to follow him.

Lief arches an eyebrow at me as someone knocks on the door. "Please, Viper. Stay here."

"Why can't I know who it is?"

"It's only going to upset you," Lief kisses my forehead. "Let me handle this, okay?"

I go back to the kitchen, but I still hear Lief. "Sir, you are not welcome here."

"My daughter is here, so I am allowed here. Let her go. I'll ... I'll pay you."

No. No. My father can't be here. He shouldn't know where we live. He shouldn't know anything about me. I made it clear how many months ago that I wanted nothing to do with him when I left him in the holding cell he was stuck in.

"Say something!" My father orders.

"You are not welcome here. You will not be coming in," Lief's voice is icy.

"Well, you can't hold my daughter hostage under the guise of marrying her. I never gave my permission, so this entire thing is ... is not real," my father argues.

I push my way toward Lief. He puts one big hand over the small of my back. I know if he doesn't like it, he can pull me back into the house and slam the door. I narrow my eyes at my dad.

He sighs. "There you are. Let's go home now, Val."

"No," I say.

"You don't have to stay with them. I have a perfectly good-"

"I'm marrying them. It's my choice. You don't need to be consulted. You're not welcome here. Stay away from me," I order him.

"You're out of your mind. They're ... they're holding you hostage, I know it," Dad accuses.

"I'd leave before my other two men show up. They don't have Lief's patience," I warn him.

"I'm not afraid of them," Dad growls before trying to grab me.

Lief pulls me back. "It's not *them* you should be afraid of. Leave the property before I call the police."

"Call them. Go ahead. I'm not doing anything wrong. I'm bringing my daughter back home where she belongs," my father insists.

I can't believe this is the same man my mother can't get enough of. He looks ragged, worn out. Lief takes out his phone. I give him the okay to call the police, but step up next to him. I can see the threat of violence in my fiancé's eyes.

"Nothing in my life is your choice. You are a part of my past and that's where you're going to stay," I warn my father. "I want that to be clear because once the police come and throw you in the back of their car, I'm going to file a restraining order against you."

"But I'm your father," he says, his jaw

slackening.

"That doesn't mean anything right now. I made it clear the last time I saw you that I never wanted to see you again. You violated that request. You've accused my fiancés of kidnapping me, and I'm not going to tolerate it," I say.

"Hello, I need to have the police come to my house, please. We have a trespasser who is threatening my fiancée," Lief says before giving the address.

My father looks at Lief, at me, then turns when he hears a car coming into the driveway. Hunter and Chase get out of the car. Lief wraps an arm around my waist. "The police will be here in five minutes. You can choose to leave with them or on your own."

"This is your last chance to avoid the police," I say. "I recommend taking it because it won't be offered again."

"I'm not afraid of the police," my dad says, puffing his chest out.

"The police are the pleasant option," Lief informs him. "Be happy I gave you two separate outs before throwing the worst case scenario at you."

"Are you threatening me? I'll be happy to share that with the-"

"I'm promising you that your daughter won't be half as kind as I'm trying to be," Lief growls. "We have enough work to do today, don't add to it."

ELEVEN

Lief

THE MAN IN FRONT OF ME IS TORN. I KNOW THAT. Some part of him believes we're holding Valerie hostage and, like any parent, he wants to protect her. However, the fact that he refuses to listen to what she's saying–every clear word leaving her lips– is an issue.

I glance at my watch. "Three minutes until the police arrive and thirty seconds until the two men behind you figure out who you are and override the options I've provided."

Tightening my arm around Valerie and pulling her against my side keeps her from being a threat. Chase and Hunter are waiting by their car. Valerie's father must recognize the limited options.

He points at me. "This isn't over."

"It is. This is my life. It is my choice what I do with it," Valerie snarls.

Her father backs away, eyes flicking between us and Hunter and Chase. He heads out and I call the police back, letting them know the man left. As I take care of that, Hunter and Chase close the distance. Hunter hugs Valerie and Chase watches her father disappear.

"Do you want us to follow him?" Chase asks.

"No," Valerie mumbles. "I want to talk to my mother. Tristan wouldn't have told my father where we live. He wouldn't have told him anything."

"Valerie," Hunter starts.

She turns her glare on him, and he puts his hands up. "Alright. I'll keep my thoughts to myself right now."

Valerie excuses herself and heads down to the gym. Chase addresses me. "He shouldn't have gotten to the front door."

"I'm aware," I agree.

"Do we need to bring back some personal security?" He presses. "I don't want any unwelcome outsider able to get this close to us and our bride-to-be."

"She won't like that," Hunter says. "It'll feel like a safe house all over again."

"And I don't like that our personal home can be accessed by people Valerie doesn't want around, and we don't know. How is that a set up for success?" Chase demands. He rubs over his forehead. "Perhaps we should let our father and Vanya move into one of his homes, and we can move into the mansion. It would be more secure."

"Let's get married to Valerie first," I suggest. "Then we can discuss-"

"We won't be able to discuss anything if her father hurts her," Chase growls. "Valerie's capable of plenty, we've seen that, but we've also seen how quickly someone's luck can run out."

"Chase," Hunter starts.

"I want to marry her and I know you do, too. To do that, we all have to make it down the aisle. I knew it had been too quiet and easy since Yuri. This is why. We've been so worried about our own enemies we haven't thought about her family and how they'd react to the marriage. We knew her father hated us and didn't approve. We didn't take it seriously and he could-"

"He's not *our* father, Chase," Hunter says.

Chase sits down and runs his hands through his hair. I haven't seen him like this before. I blink at him a few times, then make tea.

"If he was our father, she'd already be gone," Chase murmurs.

I bring over the steeping tea and set it in front of Chase. I take a breath. "Valerie isn't going to let her father interfere. If I know her, she's downstairs, beating the punching bag while practicing what she's going to say to her mother."

"We could pay off her father. Or ... something," Chase says.

"It's her problem," Hunter counters. When Chase and I both glare at him, he rolls his eyes. "Don't give me that look. Valerie likes to solve her own problems. We all know that. Give her time to process it."

Chase takes a sip of the steaming tea and exhales. "So I'm just supposed to do nothing?"

"Right now, yes," I say, agreeing with Hunter. "Let Valerie decide how to handle her family. We still need to find a new photographer and let's see if we can help with wedding plans."

We check off a few more guests and Hunter informs some of the guys that if they show up with someone after marking it's just them, their guests won't be allowed in. Chase talks a few other people down from three guests to one, and I call Konstantin and Lev.

"Security at the wedding is imperative. I trust you, Kon, to run things, but Lev, if you don't mind bringing some of your best as well, I'd appreciate it," I say.

"Are we keeping certain people out?" Kon asks.

"Of the ceremony and reception, yes. Anyone who doesn't have an invitation and/ or isn't on the list. I'll also be providing photos of individuals who are not allowed in," I explain.

"I'll need to see the venue to know how many people to bring," Lev states. "I'm still in the area on business. Are you available tomorrow?"

"Yes. I'll contact the woman I've been working

with at the venue to ensure we can scout it," I agree. "Noon?"

"Sounds good," Lev agrees.

"I'll be there," Kon assures me.

Lev leaves the call, but Konstantin lingers. "Juliana appreciated the invitation Valerie sent. She appreciates Valerie in general, but being invited meant a great deal."

"Of course," I say. I leave out the fact that he shouldn't have gotten involved with the woman he was hired to protect. I know keeping people apart is a losing battle. "You, the other men, and Juliana are very welcome to enjoy the reception, but I expect you to be on guard during the ceremony."

"No problem at all," he assures me before I hang up.

I set up a plan to get to the venue and see Chase relaxing as he talks with Hunter. I respect Chase's concern about Valerie, but I have no doubt she can handle her father. Does she want to? No. Will she? Yes.

The next day, I head to the venue with Valerie in the passenger seat. Chase doesn't want her staying home alone. Frustration radiates from her.

"Are we allowed to see your reception dress?" I ask.

"Hmm? Oh ... I don't know the rule for that. I know you're not supposed to see my wedding dress," she says with a deep sigh.

"Are you worried about your parents?" I take her hand.

"My mother admitted to telling my father. She said she thought he'd accept it and give his blessing. At least they haven't been together in person, according to Tristan," Valerie says while squeezing my hand. "Sorry for being a mess yesterday."

"You had every right to be."

"Except now Chase is worried about someone hurting me," she snorts. "My father talks a big game, but I'm not ten anymore. He can't do anything to me."

I kiss across her knuckles as we pull into the Larz Anderson House. "Seeing the venue will help. While I go over security checkpoints, you can mark areas you'd like to have photos taken on our big day. Two birds, one stone."

"We need a photographer for that," she reminds me.

I send her three website links before we get out of the car. "These three have good eyes. One of them is a photographer my parents work with for their events."

Valerie follows up on that and stays close as the woman shows us around. Zoey–that's her name. She keeps glancing at me and away. I try to ignore it. Valerie doesn't need to be jealous on top of everything else. As Lev and Konstantin look over the different entrances as pointed out by Zoey, she moves closer.

"So, you and the other two I met are marrying the same woman?" she asks.

"Yes."

"How does that work?" she asks. "Is it some kind of pact or something?"

"No. We all love her. It's simple," I state.

"It's a little odd, you have to admit. Three such attractive men who I'm sure have no problem finding women agreeing to share one instead of being able to claim the complete love and devotion of three individual women .... well ..." She moves a little closer. "It's just interesting."

"Lief," Valerie asks, while looking at something. "What's our current RSVP number at?"

"Seventy," I answer, walking towards her and leaving Zoey behind.

She taps her chin. "And how many people are supposed to be able to fit?"

"One hundred and fifty," Zoey answers, again standing too close to me.

"And we have thirty people who haven't answered, right?" Valerie continues.

"Correct. The ceremony is much smaller, as we discussed," I say, assuring her.

She rubs the back of her neck. "I'm worrying too much again, aren't I?"

"All brides worry, it's normal," Zoey says. "Especially setting up a wedding in such a short time frame. We have more availability in fall if you feel-"

"I'm marrying my husbands when I said I would," Valerie says.

Valerie walks forward, mumbling under her breath about something. Zoey sighs. "I've seen a lot of relationships end before they get down the aisle. Wedding planning is so difficult for relationships."

"I wouldn't know," I say.

"It's okay to admit that things aren't perfect in a relationship, Lief," Zoey says as her hand brushes mine. "It's basic statistics. Just under half of all marriages end in divorce. A large number of relationships end before then."

"Can you stop flirting with my fiancée?" Valerie calls loudly.

Zoey's lips part as she blushes. "I'm not flirting with-"

"Your hand is brushing his and you've been trying to make him doubt this wedding since we got here. If that's what you consider professional, I can ask someone else to help us from here on out or you can stop flirting with the man I'm marrying in less than two months," Valerie says as she turns around to look at Zoey.

"I didn't mean ... I-"

"I didn't miss it the first time we were here. I get that Lief is attractive and has plenty of allure, but he chose me and I chose him." Valerie closes the space between us and glowers at Zoey. "He's not interested in you, so your fascination ends now."

Zoey's face is bright red, but her lips tremble. "I swear, I was just stating statistics-"

"While trying to hold my fiancé's hand? Not likely. I'm not in the mood to watch him turn you down today. Walk. Away," Valerie orders.

Zoey scurries away and I pull Valerie close. "Are you jealous?"

"You're mine, Viking. I proposed. I put a ring on your finger. I'm not about to let anyone think they can have you," she huffs.

I pull Valerie close and kiss her hard, tangling my fingers in her hair. She hums, then pulls me closer. Changing the angle, I renew the kiss, sucking her tongue and nibbling her bottom lip. She pants as I draw back.

"I am yours, Valerie, as much as you're mine. People can think whatever they want, but you're the only person I'd ever let wash me in the shower, the only person I'd ever let feed me, and the only person who I'd let pick my mind," I promise.

She kisses my neck. "We should go on a date."

"Yes?" I ask.

"A private one, that ends with me tracing every one of your tattoos with my tongue," she says.

I groan and pull her close. "I don't have that kind of patience, pet."

"That's the point, Viking," shc says before kissing me again. "Also, save those sweet words for your vows."

"I'm not writing any," I say.

She pauses, then her eyes harden. "Excuse me?"

"I'm not writing anything down. I will say what I feel. I don't need to plan my promises to you. I'll give you everything that is within my power to give," I say.

Valerie groans and kisses me again. "I love you."

TWELVE

Valerie

When Lief and I get home from the venue, I wrap myself around him. He chuckles and picks me up, carrying me to the couch where he tumbles down on top of me. I kiss him hungrily. I love how blasé he is about everything, especially someone flirting with him. He doesn't care, doesn't engage, and doesn't think twice about it. It's sexy as hell.

I groan against him and suck his tongue as he grinds against me. I tug at his shirt. "Off."

"I suggested a date," he reminds me.

"Are you telling me you don't want me right now, Lief?" I ask before kissing a tattoo on his neck.

"No," he groans, gripping my hips. "I can never tell you no."

I giggle and roll him off the couch, landing on top of him. Lief rubs the back of his head, but his hand is under my knee, proof he can't help but

103

protect me. I kiss him, taking my time so he *feels* how much I love him.

"I can't wait to marry you," I say against his mouth.

He groans and pulls me tighter against his muscular body. "Valerie Prins."

Our kissing gets a lot more intense as we tug at each other's clothing. I keep calling him 'husband' until he's buried inside me. Every time he calls me Mrs. Prins, I lose my mind. Neither of us last long.

I slump on his chest when we finish. I shudder as my pussy keeps spasming around him and he groans. "You're going to make me hard again."

"Oh no, how terrible," I say sarcastically.

Lief lets me wash him in the shower, including his hair. I dry him off, then ruffle his hair with a towel. He watches me with a passive face, but there's a softness to his eyes as I keep fluffing his hair.

I sit on his lap and kiss him again. "I love you, Lief. So much."

He strokes my back and kisses the inside of my shoulder. "I love you, Valerie. It doesn't matter to me if someone flirts. It does nothing. Especially compared to when *you* flirt with me."

How am I not supposed to love him when he says things like that?

We have a good night together. When Hunter and Chase get home, they join us in the movie marathon. The guys take turns feeding me popcorn and snacks as we laugh and joke around. It feels good. It feels *normal.*

The next morning, I wake up curled around Chase with Hunter hugging my back. Lief is asleep on his own, at peace. I get up, trying to sneak out, but Hunter jerks me back down. "Where do you think you're going?"

"I was going to make breakfast," I murmur.

"I'm not ready for you to leave," Hunter says, wrapping himself around me again. "I like cuddling you, so stay here. Just a little longer."

I roll over and hug him, kissing across his chest. "Is something wrong, Hunt?"

"Chase is all worried about you. You spent all yesterday with Lief. Am I slipping through the cracks?"

"No," I answer, sucking his neck. "I love you, Hunt. Do you want to go on another date? We could do plenty of things, wedding related and non-wedding related."

"We should pick out some clothes for the honeymoon. Things I'm allowed to tear off you," he murmurs in my ear.

I roll my eyes. I know he's hard. He's hard every morning. I take his hand and drag him into the bathroom with me. We brush our teeth. When I see him pick up speed, I try to finish first. I win and turn around to face him, sticking out my tongue just for him to lick it.

Hunter jerks me against him and kisses me. The

mint adds an extra layer to our kiss that I didn't expect. He presses his forehead to mine. "I love you so much, Dorogaya."

"We could run away together today. Forget all about any work you have to do and make the most of our Sunday," I offer.

"Chase would lose his mind," Hunter sighs.

"Why?"

"Your father," he sighs. "Chase is all worried about him taking you away or hurting you."

I roll my eyes. "He's lost so much of himself because of drinking. I don't know what his memory is like, I don't know-"

Hunter covers my mouth. "That's the problem. There's too much we don't know. None of us like not knowing."

"Good to know those control issues haven't budged," I say against his palm.

"I know you're sassing me," he pulls his hand away and kisses me again. "How about we get your mother, Vanya, and Josefine together and have a conversation about things?"

"Josefine is taking care of some business in Denmark. She won't be back until the end of the week," I mumble.

"We'll set it up for then," he decides.

Hunter and I go out for lunch, but he insists on leaving a note for Chase and Lief. I go on a date with Chase, trying to shake some worry off him with laser tag. It doesn't seem to help. Even after beating everyone else, I can tell he's brooding.

"Chase, everything's going to be okay. We're all going to be at the altar. You guys will be each other's best men, and we'll find the officiant," I promise as we head home.

"I'm not willing to take the risk that we're overlooking some danger as far as you're concerned," he grumbles.

"You can't control everything, even if we all wish we could. Sometimes, we just have to believe things will turn out correctly," I say. "I'm not letting anything in this world keep me from marrying you three."

Chase looks at me for a long moment, then sighs. "I know it seems ridiculous, but you matter to me. I know my name doesn't invite a lot of friends and with your parents not approving of this-"

"I'm getting all the moms together to talk to them when Josefine gets back. My mom is either going to get on board or be kept in the dark. Those are the only two options, okay?" I ask.

He sighs. "It'll have to do."

When we pull into the driveway, I climb onto his lap. "You love me, right?"

"Of course I do, baby doll."

"And you trust me," I say as I undo some buttons on his shirt.

"Yes," he agrees.

"Trust me now. I will be at that altar. After

everything we've been through, everything we've survived, I'm expecting you three to be there, too. We'll get married, have a fun and exhausting reception, then fly to Rio to enjoy a luxurious honeymoon with no worries at all," I swear.

He presses his forehead to mine. "You're too convincing for your own good."

"You know it helps," I argue, kissing his lips.

The next day Lief and I get our date—walking through a museum together as we exchange fun facts—and then it's the weekend.

We meet for lunch and get the V.I.P. room for some privacy. Josefine gushes about the venue and the invitations, telling me how excited she is, while Vanya's more withdrawn. She shrugs. "Hunter hasn't spoken to me since we were all wedding planning at the mansion. I don't believe he wants me there."

"You two have been making a lot of progress, but it is a process, Vanya. He's not used to being mothered, doesn't know how to cope with it, and he's not the same little boy you left. It will take time for you two," I assure her.

My mother walks in, her eyes bloodshot and tired. She sits between Josefine and Vanya before giving a nervous smile. My face loses its warmth. I know it right away. Vanya gives me a proud smile, then leans back.

"Mother, is there a reason you told your husband where I live?" I ask.

She pales. "He ... he just asked how you were, if you were still being held hostage. I said you were never a hostage. I don't know how, but I thought if you could just prove that you weren't, he'd be done and ..."

"He showed up! He tried to take me from Lief. We had to threaten him with the police," I say, leaving out the other threats.

"I'm sorry," she replies. "I just.."

"And you told him about me getting married. I didn't tell him for a reason. I hesitated to tell *you*. In case you forgot, it was my fiancés who reached out to you," I remind her. "Your husband isn't welcome at my wedding. He's not getting an invitation and you're not getting a plus one."

"Well ..." she adjusts. "It's not a real wedding."

Josefine and Vanya both gape at my mother. She shrugs, but shrinks a little. "It's not. One wedding is real, and the rest is for show. You can't marry three men. It's impossible and there's no way around that. One woman. One man."

I grit my teeth. "This is why you're only invited to the reception."

Her eyes water. "What!"

"I refuse to have anyone at the ceremony who doesn't support *all three* of my husbands and me. They tried to tell me you'd changed, that you'd accept this, that you could see me as more than a greedy slut, but they were wrong."

A tear runs down my mother's cheek, but it does

nothing to me. She huffs and shakes her head. "You can't marry three men! It's illegal! You marry one, then the other two are just ... mistresses!"

"Tina." Josefine puts a hand to her chest. "You can't possibly think that."

"I want to be proud of being your mother, but I'm not. Maybe if I would have left your father, you wouldn't have these kinds of issues," my mother says. "Don't worry. I won't ruin your happy day by being there."

"Good," I say.

She pauses, looks at me with obvious hurt, and I shrug. "I will not change everything in my life to satisfy you. I don't need your validation to be happy. I've lived without you since I was sixteen. Going back to no-contact won't be hard."

She storms off before we can even get our drinks. I take a few slow breaths. Hunter wouldn't be proud of me, Chase wouldn't either. That's fine. I can be the brat right now because it means my grooms won't have to deal with being looked down upon. I can shoulder my parents' judgment.

"Valerie," Josefine says while taking my hand. "I'm proud of you."

I force my lips into a firm line.

"It's no wonder you're so at home in the mansion. You know how to make things happen and how to control meetings," Vanya whispers.

I swallow and take the menu. "So, I'm assuming you're doing mother and groom dances?"

"Probably not," Vanya says.

"There's no reason to set aside special time for that." Josefine shrugs. "Especially if you're not doing something like that. I'll dance with Lief whenever he pleases."

Vanya nods.

"Are either of you ... do you have reservations about me marrying all the guys?" I ask without meeting their eyes.

"No, Valerie. I see how Lief is with you. His happiness is all that matters. He's never smiled so much in his life," Josefine says.

"I worried about you not wanting a life in their business, but I never questioned your choice to be with my sons or Lief. You four are already a family. Anyone who's met you, anyone who's seen you all together, knows it," Vanya agrees.

"We're on your side, sweetheart. I'm excited to call you my daughter soon," Josefine insists.

She's *excited* to have me as a daughter. That's worth more than being connected to someone out of obligation. And that's what I'm going to hold onto.

THIRTEEN

Hunter

OUT OF ALL THE PREPARATION FOR THE WEDDING over the last five weeks, I thought the bachelor party would be my favorite part. However, as I get ready, I notice Valerie is just sitting in the tub. No bubbles, no candles, just sitting there, staring at the ceiling with the lights low.

"Aren't you having your bachelorette party tonight?"

"Yeah," she murmurs.

She's been a little off for the last few weeks, but I assumed it was the stress of wedding planning and working while also taking care of us. Now, I don't know. I sit on the floor beside her and take her hand, kissing just above the ring I got her. "You don't sound very excited."

"And you're not rushing out the door," she answers.

"Shockingly, strippers are less exciting than my

fiancée," I say, feeling my brow furrow. "Did your father try something?"

"He's been silent."

"What's bothering you?"

"Nothing's bothering me Hunt, go have fun with Lief and Chase and everyone else. Make those strippers rich tonight," she encourages before giving me a damp kiss on the cheek.

I don't move. I continue watching Valerie, but she doesn't give in like normal. Hell, I learned the shut up and watch trick from her, so I shouldn't be surprised that she's immune, but I can tell her head is somewhere else.

"Something's bothering you. I'm not leaving until you tell me," I say.

"Lief and Chase will leave without you."

"I don't care," I take off my coat, eyeing her bath. "I'm five seconds from getting in. Want to count them down?"

"Hunter, don't."

"Five." I start, pulling at my shirt. "Four." I get enough buttons undone to pull it over my head. "Three."

"I uninvited my mother from the wedding," she says with a groan before sinking deeper. Only her eyes remain over the cloudy water.

I sigh and sit on the edge of the tub. "Why?"

Valerie blows some bubbles, and I reach for my belt when she pops back up. "Because she doesn't support our marriage! She said it in front of your mom and Josefine. She called you and Chase my mistresses. I called her last week to see if she's changed her mind after talking to Sophia, and my mother still said I was making a mockery of marriage by claiming three men. It started a fight. We both ... said things."

"That you meant," I fill in.

"She can't say I'm making a mockery of marriage when she married my father and still won't leave him after what he did to Tristan and me. Our marriage will be real and right. I love all three of you. You love me. You'd never hurt me, raise a hand against me, abuse my trust or love. So she's full of shit and she doesn't get to be at my wedding when she's going to be terrible about it," Valerie huffs before crossing her arms.

I text Chase and Lief to leave without me, then take Valerie's hand. I play with her fingers. "Why didn't you tell me?"

"Because I'm supposed to be a good example. I know that you and Vanya aren't close, and I know that you still have issues with her, so why would you keep working on that when I'm cutting my mother out of my life again?" she whispers.

I chuckle and pull her closer to me. "Dorogaya, our relationships with our mothers are complicated and different. You've made the same effort you're asking me to make with my mother. And you're reaffirming those boundaries you're so fond of."

"Yeah, but I didn't take the high road."

"It's overrated," I say.

"You have a bachelor's party. Go," she encourages again.

I take a breath, then sink into the tub, leaving my shoes hanging out. Valerie gapes at me. "Hunter Volkov, you still have pants on!"

"I'd rather stay here and make you feel better, cuddle you, kiss you, spend all night with you than go throw ones," I say. "You're more important."

Valerie softens, then turns, so she's sitting the wrong way in the tub, just like me, her legs hanging out over the edge. "I love you, Krolik."

"I'm very loveable," I say, chuckling.

"I mean it. You're a good man, even if you're beyond frustrating sometimes."

She leans her head on my shoulder.

I wrap an arm around her and press my lips to her forehead. "I'll frustrate you forever."

"Softy," she grumbles.

I laugh with her until Chase and Lief come in. Valerie explains the situation. My brother and Lief both offer to stay, but she shakes her head. "We made plans. We're sticking to them. Sophia, Juliana, Elaine, and Danny will be here soon enough. I know the guys are waiting for you."

"Are you sure, baby doll?" Chase asks.

"Very," Valerie sighs. "Now all three of you, out. I know what will happen if you see me naked."

"We'll throw hundreds at you?" I tease.

She rolls her eyes. "Go have fun. I'm serious."

I stay a moment longer, make sure our fiancée is serious, then change. We get into a limo, but I can't quite force a smile. Lief nudges me. "Valerie's strong. She talked about it, so she'll feel better."

"It didn't use to take her so long to share when something was bothering her," I grumble. "Did she tell you guys about her mother?"

"No," Chase answers. "I thought getting married was supposed to bring us closer together."

"It will," Lief says. "Right now, it's constant stress, but once we get to the wedding, things will calm down. We've made all our backup plans, we've finished the seating chart, got the officiant, all we have left to do is the walk, right?"

Chase nods. "I've written my vows."

I haven't. Shit. I knew I was forgetting something. How am I supposed to organize my thoughts or focus on one thing? I'm going after Chase! I can't have *nothing* because I know he's going to pull out his sweet side and make her all gooey, so I have to live up to that and Lief.

"You still have time to write yours," Lief reminds him.

"Did you?"

"I told her I don't need to write down what I feel for her. What I feel, I feel constantly," Lief says dismissively.

Before I can argue, we pull up to the club. Lev, Konstantin, and a few of the other high-ranking business associates are there. Plus, Gunner. The rest of the guys were invited, so they're either inside, or didn't want to leave the kids.

Gunner pats my chest. "Turn that frown upside down! It's party time!"

We get the V.I.P. room and throw plenty of money to the strippers. When Lev insists I get a lap dance, I nod to the woman and let her dance on me, giving her money as she does. Gunner chuckles.

"I've never seen you bored around strippers, Hunter," Gunner teases.

"Considering the woman I'm marrying, this is not exciting," I admit.

"Oh, so you get lap dances often?" Konstantin asks.

When I shoot him a look, he swallows. "Sir."

"I get much better than lap dances," I say.

"Well, I know the girls are going all out tonight," Holden says as he joins us. "Sophia asked a hundred times if it was okay to see male strippers."

Jealousy eats at me, but I take a slow breath. Two days until we're married.

Lief gives a stripper a ten, putting it between her teeth. His face is as impassive as ever until he nods to Kon and goes to get drinks.

Chase is enjoying himself. He's already five drinks in, dancing on the pole with the ladies. I take a picture of him as the women try to teach him what to do.

"Just relax," Roman says, as he hands me some

bourbon. "Celebrate that it's the last night you're a bachelor."

"That's a better way to look at it," I agree. "I can kiss all those tabloid stories goodbye. No more playboy mentality. A good woman to call mine!"

Chase cheers with me. I lose myself in the women, the guys laughing, and we have plenty of fun on and off the dance floor until we're in front of expensive, well cooked, seasoned steak. I moan and can't resist devouring it.

Lief looks sober, but Chase is already sleeping at the table.

Lev shakes his head. "Just reminds me I need to get married when young or not at all."

"Are you calling us old Vasily Lev?" I demand.

He winks at me and wishes me strength in Russian before downing another shot.

After we eat and sober up somewhat with the food, we end up going to another club. Chase and I dance on the bar, throwing money for women who dance with us or near us. Some flash their tits, but it doesn't do much for me ... other than make me miss Valerie.

I want to crash her party, remind her why she loves us, and break one of the few rules tonight.

I grab Lief. "We should find out where our fiancée is."

"Two clubs over," he says. "We promised we wouldn't rejoin her until morning, then we'd pick up our tuxes and spend tomorrow night apart, too."

"Fuck that. I don't want a single night without her!" Chase yells before turning to the crowd. "I'm getting married!"

People cheer, but Lev shakes his head. He's me twenty years ago, unwilling to admit love has a place in our world, convinced it's a weakness. Kon, however, is texting.

I hop down, stumble and nearly take out a woman. Two, hold me up and guide me to Kon as I point the way. I see flashes, but assume it's the lights until I'm standing in front of Kon.

"Thank you, ladies. My fiancée thanks you," I say, chuckling.

"Hunter, are you nauseous?" Kon asks.

I pat his chest. "You miss your girlfriend. It's cute."

He blushes and clears his throat. "I'm fine."

"Who ya texting, then?" I ask, slurring my words and speaking a dizzying mix of Russian and English.

"I mean, I'm texting her, but ..."

"We should crash their party!" I insist.

"I was given strict orders to stay sober and to keep you three from doing that," Konstantin stands firm.

"Who orders you? Lief? He's not head of security anymore. You are."

"I miss Valerie," Chase grumbles. "I don't want these other women. I want my baby doll wrapped around me."

I motion to Chase. "The boss is being very clear."

"There are rules." Roman grabs the scruff of my shirt. "You're not joining her tonight."

"I'm the boss!" Chase huffs. "You will take me to my bride."

Holden shakes his head and half-carries Chase to a booth. Lief hops down from the bar like its nothing. He stumbles a bit as he stands and blinks a few times. "I'm drunk."

"Congrats, giant," I say. "Let's get our woman."

"It's Valerie that ordered me to keep you apart." Konstantin crosses his massive arms over his chest.

"So? Chase and I are the bosses. We want her. We're going to get her. All you have to do is stay here. We're plenty capable."

I head toward the door, but Roman doesn't let go.

Konstantin blocks my path. "She gave an order. I've seen what happens to people who cross her. Jail or dead. I'm not on that list."

"You fear my bride more than me?" I ask.

"Smart," Lief points at Konstantin, then hugs him. "You've learned so much. I'm proud."

Konstantin goes bright red again. "Um ... thank you?"

"So proud. I remember when you were little and nervous. Now you're all bulky and strong. Such a good man. You should be proud of yourself. I am."

Roman sighs. "Konstantin, are you able to get free?"

He shakes his head.

Roman whistles, and Gunner appears. I'm passed to the second man as Roman adjusts his shirt. "Hold on to him. They're all drunk. We're getting a hotel."

"Food?" Lief asks.

"I'm getting Valerie!"

"Tomorrow," Roman calls before heading out.

Then everything goes blurry.

FOURTEEN

Valerie

I swat the stripper's ass as he grinds on me and he jumps, covering his butt and wagging his finger at me. "I thought you were supposed to be nice."

"I never said that," I tease.

Sophia giggles and throws more ones before she realizes she's out. She reaches into her wallet and I catch her hand. "Hold up there."

"This is so much fun!"

"Don't start throwing the big bills," I tease. I look at the soda in her glass, then touch her stomach. She jumps, then laughs. I rub her flat belly. "I can't believe there's a baby growing in here."

"I can't believe you're pregnant at a bachelorette party!" Danny teases as she slides a five into another guy's speedo. She winks at him.

Elaine gets up to dance with the guys, and Juliana adjusts one of the Pomeranians in her lap. She glances at her phone and waves the guy away.

I arch my eyebrow at her. "Not up to your speed?"

"You've seen my sexy men. As glorious as these guys are and how well they move, I have specific tastes," Juliana insists. "I know my worth."

Of course, then the guys want to impress her, until they ask who the bride to be is. Considering how drunk Elaine is and how much fun she's having, I almost point at her, but Danny puts both my hands up.

"Here she is, boys, and she's no stranger to having three men. Rock her world," Danny says.

I gape at her, but then I'm given a private Magic Mike show. I see Sophia recording and giggling. I have to admit, the guys are hot, and the way they're moving on me is so sexy, I'm wishing I would have hopped on Hunter when he was in the tub with me.

I'm let up, fan myself, and sigh as I stroke over one of the guy's pecks. He makes his chest bounce under my touch.

The clubs, dinner, the pole dancing class we took, all of it pales in comparison to this.

"Uh-oh," Sophia says before jumping up and grabbing my hand. "Danny, evasion!"

"Done, Juliana, can you-"

"Oh, I'm so ready for fun," she says with a wicked smile. "Guys, I think Elaine is very eager for some of your magic.

Sophia leads me out the back and into Gunner.

He's panting. He points at me. "Lief is *never* allowed to get drunk again."

"What's going on?" I ask. "Sophia, should you be running?"

"Please, I have four husbands to keep up with. This is nothing," she assures me.

"What happened with Lief?" I ask, then realize I've never seen him drunk. He's drank plenty, but he's only ever been tipsy around me. "Is he okay? Is he hurt?"

"He put Kon in a choke hold and teased him until Hunter slipped away. Apparently, you're better than strippers, the most expensive steak the world offers, and partying with friends," Gunner informs me. "I'd give you props if you weren't such a distraction."

"Are my men okay?" I demand.

"You're not drunk enough," Gunner says before handing me a flask.

I narrow my eyes, drain it, then hand it back. "My fiancé's better be in one piece and still gorgeous when we get to the venue in two days."

"Right now, they're all free of bruises, but they're determined to grab you and carry you home," Gunner pants.

Sophia hugs him. "You did your best, gorgeous."

"They're belligerent. Also, paparazzi happened, so there will be some unflattering pictures. Hunter, being held up by two women, will be one of them," Gunner informs.

I sigh and rub my forehead. "Great."

I hear police sirens and point at Gunner. "Go make sure that's not for my men and tell them I went home. They'll go happily."

"I think Lief is tracking your phone," Gunner answers.

I take his face between my hands. "Gun, they're drunk. How hard can it be to give them all one more drink so they pass out and then you can drag them into a limo and leave them on the couch or floor. I have faith in you. Use the muscles Sophia says you have and take care of my grooms to make sure they show up at the altar."

Gunner looks from me to Sophia. I turn his chin back to me. "Are you going to let Roman steal the spotlight and save the day?"

He points at me. "That's a dirty ploy."

"I'm just saying."

He hurries off and Sophia sighs. "You like to stir trouble, don't you?"

"I just know what works. Gunner is still threatened by Roman, so all I have to do is hint. I'd send you to get it done, but then your husbands will get distracted. Let's go to a hotel," I suggest.

Sophia texts Juliana, Danny, and Elaine as she and I head to the suite we booked. I sigh as I fall back on the plush bed, then my phone rings. It's Lief.

I groan and roll onto my belly. "Hi, Viking, are you having fun?"

"You're not at home," he accuses.

"No, but you are, so get some rest for me."

"We want *you*," he growls.

"You'll get me after our wedding day. We all agreed it would be a special night, so that's what we're going to do. Behave and you'll have kinky fun with me after we say, I do," I say.

"I don't like this. You should be here. I'll come find you," he decides.

"Lief Prins, if you leave the house, I'm going to the courthouse and marry Chase," I say.

He's silent.

"You're supposed to be the logical one. Tell me the stats for drinking and driving where things end well," I order.

Again, he says nothing.

"Tell me the odds of us getting married if you're in the hospital," I say, softer.

"None," he whispers.

"Stay home. Keep Hunter and Chase with you, then sleep it off. I will see you three tomorrow to get my things from the house. We'll kiss, love on each other, then part ways until after the wedding, just like we planned. And we planned it for a good reason, didn't we?"

"Da," he answers.

"I love you and I want to marry you. I want to sign our marriage certificate and take your last name. I want to enjoy all three of you in two days, from our vows to the party to the start of our honeymoon. I can't do that if you're hurt," I say.

He sighs. "I want to fall asleep to you braiding my hair, Viper. Why are you so far away?"

"Is that our woman?" Hunter demands. "Dorogaya, come-"

The call drops. I roll my eyes. Sophia laughs as she sits next to me. "Let me guess, they're a mess without you?"

I smile. "I get it, though. I'm tempted to run back home right now and take care of them."

"Really?" Sophia arches an eyebrow. "You want to go take care of your three grown fiancés because they're drunk?"

"No," I huff, then rub my arm. "I want to take care of them because they're mine. I want to love on them, hug them, kiss them, get them in pajamas and cuddle them to sleep."

"I can't believe you're sappy," Sophia giggles. "What happened to my best friend?"

I blush and hit her with a pillow. "You shush! I got Konstantin to ignore Lief's orders. Do you know what a win that is? It means I'm scary."

"Sure you are," she teases. "The strippers thought so too. Want to see the videos?"

"Sophia Agosti, you better delete those right now!"

We wrestle for her phone and she laughs and squeals until Danny comes in. She rolls her eyes.

"Juliana was stolen by Kon and Elaine got in a cab, determined to shower in her own apartment."

I throw myself on the bed. "You're both married ... does it get easier to be away from your husbands?"

"I might love Massimo, but I don't always like him," Danny mumbles.

Sophia gives her a look and Danny rolls her eyes. "No, it doesn't. Even when we fight, I'd rather be yelling at him and giving him sass, seeing the growing love and lust in his eyes every time we get frustrated than pouting off on my own."

"Which is why I saw him in the hallway right before Valerie and I got here, right?" Sophia asks.

Danny flips her off, but laughs. "Yes. I couldn't just leave my husband and baby in Italy. He's in the room next door."

I laugh.

"Sophia's husbands are just down the hall, so I don't want to hear it," Danny huffs.

"Let me guess–Link is with Nick?" I ask.

"Nick didn't feel the need to join a bachelor party," Sophia says. She doesn't make any move to leave. "Sometimes being apart from my husbands is nice. It's good to remember that I'm my own person, not just a wife or mother, even though I love being both."

"Well then, I'm not wrong for being tempted to go see them," I mumble.

We pamper ourselves as much as we can in our

room, but soon enough, Sophia and Danny fall asleep. I have zero illusions they'll stay here all night when their families are so close. Still, I make a fake 'me' out of pillows, pull the blanket up, then grab my phone.

It's not too late, only one a.m.

I call one of the security guys and have them take me home. The man asks a few questions, namely why the guys aren't with me, but I snap at him, reminding him who I am and he's quiet for the rest of the ride.

I get out, open the door at home, and tiptoe around the house. The guy named Lev sleeps on the couch, but doesn't stir as I head upstairs. My guys are spread across the bed, not touching each other, wearing only their boxers. I shake my head and take off my shoes. I stumble, glance up, and find Lief's eyes on me.

He smiles and opens his arms to me. I climb on the bed and sit on his lap, stroking through his hair before kissing him.

"You couldn't resist," he murmurs.

"I waited until after midnight. It's tomorrow," I say.

"Not morning, pet. You caved," he says before hugging me and kissing my forehead. "Missed you."

"You didn't have fun?"

"We didn't want strippers, we wanted you," he sighs, inhaling my hair. "You're better."

A pillow smacks me. "Shut up, Lief. If you're calling her again-"

I grab the pillow and pull. Chase rolls over, sees me, then pries me from Lief, cuddling me close. "No more nights alone."

"We're not supposed to spend tomorrow night together," I say.

Lief rolls and hugs me from behind. "Too bad."

"Is Hunt-"

"You missed the messy parts," Chase sighs. "He needs to sleep, trust me."

I kiss him, then turn and kiss Lief. "I love you both. Thank you for behaving."

"Telling me not to come get you, then you come here," Lief grumbles.

"I wasn't drunk, and I took a car instead of driving," I say. "Now we're all in one piece and-"

"Mine," Hunter lies on top of me, squishing me. Lief and Chase both complain about his elbows and I roll onto my back so Hunter's more comfortable.

Chase huffs, but pushes Hunter down until he's using my belly as a pillow so Chase can rest his head on my chest.

"I like that you always come back to us," he sighs before sleep takes him back.

Lief kisses me and slides his arm under my head. "Our beautiful bride."

I fall asleep, happy, basking in the love of all three of my men.

FIFTEEN

Chase

I wake up smelling Valerie's perfume. I'd been sure that it had been a dream, that she hadn't joined us. It was one of three rules. She'd said we weren't allowed to do anything with the strippers that we wouldn't want her to do with someone else. Number two was no paparazzi. Number three was staying separate until morning. She broke rule three.

Opening my eyes, I find her asleep, her head resting on mine until I move. She turns her head and her arm tightens around Hunter, who's sleeping on her belly. Lief strokes through Valerie's hair with a smile.

I open my mouth, but he puts a finger to his lips. I roll my eyes. I'm over having the title of 'boss' and not getting my way. I get up and get through a much needed shower, trying to wash my hangover down the drain.

A few minutes later, I'm joined by Valerie. She strokes over my body and kisses my neck. "Good morning, baby boy."

"You're naughty, breaking rules when we were manhandled here," I grumble.

She arches an eyebrow at me. "I thought I was being sweet, but I'll just get out and-"

I pull her against me, her ass rubbing my hard cock. I shudder and press my forehead against her shoulder. "You're not getting out without a very hard punishment."

"Hard, huh?" she rubs her ass against me. "I thought we agreed on no sex leading up to the wedding."

"Oral isn't sex," I say seriously.

"Depends on if it's done right," she teases.

Still, she drops to her knees, wrapping her hand around my cock as she watches me. She strokes, eroding my resolve every time her hand tightens around me. I thrust into her hand. "Are you going to use your hands on me, baby doll?"

"I'm thinking about more, but if I get you started, you're going to want to do the same. We both know where that will lead," she murmurs.

"You have no faith in me," I say, even though I'm planning what she described. I will not let her make me come without returning the favor.

"And once you get started, Lief and Hunter will want a turn. How can I be sure we don't end up having sex?"

"So what if we do?" I ask, softening a groan. "I thought you enjoyed having sex with us."

"I do," she answers before licking across the head of my cock. "But I want our wedding night to be special."

"It'll be special because we'll be married," I argue.

Valerie stands up and taps my nose. "Now who's being naughty?"

I press her against the wall and kiss her. Grabbing Valerie's full ass, I grind against her, thrusting my cock between her thighs. Valerie shudders and grips my shoulders. "Baby boy, I-"

"You came home because you wanted to be with us," I remind her against her lips. "So be with us."

She moans and kisses me deeper, wrapping her arms around my neck as she rubs herself against me. I run my nose along hers, then grip her hair. "Yes or no, baby doll. Do you want to come for my cock or for my fingers?"

"Both, always both," she breathes. "You ruin me."

"Good," I growl as I lift her thigh over my hip and slam into her. She tries to cover her mouth, tries to hide what we're doing, but I pry her hand off her mouth. "Oh no, you opened the doors. It's not fair if Hunter and Lief don't get to have you, too."

"Chase!" she yells as I fuck her harder. Valerie

claws my shoulders as she tries to move with me, taking me the way she needs.

I squeeze her thigh and bite her bottom lip as her pussy tightens around my cock. She's so wet, so tight, so perfect as she meets every thrust and kisses me between her moans. I can't wait for her to promise me forever, forever loving her, forever having her just like this, no moderation, no restraint, just us, going at it like we need this to survive.

"Fuck," I hiss.

Valerie whimpers and pulls me tighter against her. "I'm so close, Chase. Please!"

I increase the pace, slamming into her again and again as I kiss her neck, give her soft nibbles, pull her hair and swat her thigh. She comes apart, digging her teeth into my chest to quiet the howl of pleasure that leaves her throat.

I draw back, but Valerie just sinks to her knees and wraps her mouth around my cock, sucking as she grips my ass, jerking me further down her throat. I groan and hold her hair in my hands. "Good girl. You know just what I need."

She moans and rolls her whole body towards me to take more of my length down her throat. Hunter watches from the doorway, eager to do more than watch. I nod to him and he joins us in a second, lifting our fiancée and sliding under her so he can fuck her.

Valerie gasps and glances back at Hunter. He

squeezes her breast. "I'm sure you're not ignoring Chase for me."

"You're just as naughty as he is," she pants. "Krolik, please!"

He's rushing her, I can tell, pounding into her, while holding her hips in place. Her eyes flutter. Then he stops, his arms shaking. "Blow him while I fuck you or I won't fuck you at all."

Valerie lets out a little whine, then turns, taking me down her tight throat again. Every intense suck that hollows her red cheeks, the way her lips work over my length and her wicked tongue drives me insane. I don't know how to stay focused on anything but her.

Bracing myself on the wall, I try to hold out, but her eyes close and she moans around my cock. It pushes me over the edge. I grip her hair, jerk her further forward, and grunt as I come down her throat.

She hums and laps at the head of my cock until I jerk away, far too sensitive to let her continue. She pushes against Hunter. "I can't! I can't, I'm gonna-"

He jerks her down hard. "Come for me, now, Dorogaya. Right now."

Valerie's eyes roll back as she grips Hunter's hands on her. Her toes curl as her back arches. She's so damn beautiful. I could watch her come all day every day and still want more of her.

Hunter lifts her, and I pull her to her feet. She trembles. Hunter grips his cock, stroking. "I'm assuming we're only allowed to come in your mouth today?"

"Yes," she trembles as she answers him. "That's the rule."

"You shouldn't make rules just to break them," Lief says.

He's been watching. I'm sure of that based on how frustrated he looks. Not to mention, he's naked. Valerie pants as she glances at him. She swallows. "I ... this isn't a rule I can break."

"Oh yes you can," Hunter and I disagree.

Still, Lief grabs her hips, pulls her feet out of the shower and thrusts into her, bending her over so she takes Hunter down her throat. Lief strokes her back as Hunter fists her hair. Valerie's loud all the same, moaning and panting. Lief adjusts and fucks her faster, setting the pace she uses to blow Hunter.

"Fuck, such a good morning," Hunter moans.

"We will not manage any kind of meeting in the morning with her," I chuckle.

I finish my shower just as Valerie finishes with Hunter. She nearly falls when Lief lightens his hold. Rather than returning her to the shower, he carries her to bed. I glance over as I pull my pants on. Valerie rolls onto her belly to blow Lief.

He swats her ass, but Hunter fixes that. He gives her a hard swat and chuckles. "Naughty girl."

Her reply is muffled around Lief's cock as he takes control, fucking her mouth the way she likes it. He shakes, groans, then comes, bracing himself on Valerie's lower back as he softens his breathing and the light grunts that follow every little move of his hips.

"We're marrying the best woman possible," I say to Hunter as he gets dressed.

"I agree, but can you say it a little softer? Coming doesn't fix a hangover," he whispers.

I chuckle and Valerie pants. Lief picks her up. "Let's go. I have demands."

"Viking, you just ... what else could you ... ugh, no!" she complains as Lief picks her up and carries her to the bathroom. "I'll make sure she gets back to her bridesmaids."

I hear water falling again and then Valerie. "You were serious?"

"You're the only one I let do this. Not even my mother gets to," he answers.

I share a look with Hunter and he peeks in. I follow, and we see Valerie stroking through Lief's hair, washing it.

"You wouldn't let her braid your hair?" Valerie asks before kissing Lief's back.

"No, pet. Only you."

"What a softie. Are you sure that's the guy who used to carry out hits?" Hunter asks.

"I can hear you," Lief calls. "Want to talk about how we fought over Valerie's attention last night, or are you two going to your last tux fitting?"

Hunter huffs. "Someone isn't satisfied with one orgasm."

Before Lief can follow up on that, Hunter hurries downstairs to make coffee. Valerie whispers something to Lief and strokes his back. A part of me is still jealous she's marrying him on paper and taking his last name, but I know it makes sense.

Lief comes down a little later with his hair dried and a braid flowing in his hair just behind his ear. Valerie sighs. "Alright, I have to get back to the girls. No over-drinking today. We all have to look nice for tomorrow."

"And we're not seeing you again until tomorrow?" I'm guessing.

She kisses me. "You got more out of me today than you were supposed to."

"Won't change the fact you're not leaving the wedding venue until we've all had our way with you," Hunter says.

She blushes and takes a few deep breaths. "I can't believe we did it. We've made it here. Minimal problems, all issues resolved, no one hurt."

"Just like you promised me," I remind her, pulling Valerie close and kissing her. "Stop jinxing our wedding. Wait until we all get down the aisle."

"I can't wait," she says, hugging me tight. "It doesn't matter what happens tomorrow, as long as we end up together, saying "I do" and cutting that cake."

"Hunter?" I ask, leaning back to him as Valerie kisses Lief.

"Yeah, I got the small one for us to pick at and I

let that new little protégé of Lief's know that he better be willing to get us food during the reception in case we get caught up talking," Hunter says. "We don't need our wife hangry."

Wife.

I love the word. I love thinking of Valerie as ours. She looks over at us and bites her bottom lip. I can tell she's thinking the same things.

"Stay armed," I say.

She rolls her eyes. "I always am. But you better make sure security is taken care of. If I have to use your father's engagement present on my wedding day, I'm going to be very upset."

"I love her," Hunter says, sighing. "Willing to kick ass while in some kind of white formal gown."

"That's our woman," I agree.

SIXTEEN

Valerie

LESS THAN TWENTY-FOUR HOURS UNTIL I'M GETTING married. Of course, today is a pampering day after the waxing appointment, which is kind of hellish. I walk like an old Western Movie sheriff and glare at Sophia.

"You said it wasn't painful," I growl.

"And you've dealt with worse things. Want to rehash you being kidnapped?" She narrows her eyes.

"It was just twice," I say, as I wave it away.

Sophia turns me around. "Twice?"

"Yeah, once when I found out what the guys did, one of the security guys thought I was a threat and held me hostage. I had it taken care of by the time the guys got there and ... finished it," I say, sparing her the details. "And then by Hunter and Chase's aunt, who wanted revenge. They took me after almost beating Hunter to death and I ... well,

I'm not proud of the tactics I used, but it kept all my men alive and got her arrested and that 'business' taken care of."

The blatant horror in Sophia's eyes has me rethinking those experiences. How many people have I seen hurt, beaten, or killed since meeting my men? Too many. I nibble my bottom lip as I grab her hand and drag her to the spa we're meeting the girls at. We all need some relaxing. A massage, seaweed wrap, sauna, and some skin care will do us good.

"I always knew you were fierce, but ... how can you just brush that off?" Sophia asks as we get massages.

Elaine has headphones in and Danny is limp, probably asleep. Julianna's in a private room all to herself. I sigh. "I didn't, but the fact that my fiancés survived was all that was important. It tripped me up a bit after each, but it proved how much I can handle. I felt strong. I still feel strong."

"Because of your men or you?" Sophia probes.

"Me. Knowing that I'm capable of so much, that I can handle myself, protect the men I love and myself, and do it with or without a weapon makes me feel like I can take on anything. It didn't stop me from reacting when I saw my dad, but ... I have the confidcncc I always wanted growing up," I whisper. "Back when I just used my attitude as a weapon instead of being able to back it up."

"You've never been the 'all talk, no bite' type,

Val. Don't change that," Sophia says, while turning to look at me.

I give her a smile. Then we enjoy being pampered. We end our trip in a jacuzzi. After all the treatments, the waxing appointment is forgotten. I don't feel any of the pain I did when we left. I sigh.

"So, any regrets before getting married?" Danny asks. "Making a list of famous people you'd like to use a hall pass for?"

"No," I say. "Well ... I think a part of me wishes my parents were better people so I could have a few more traditions in the wedding, but that's it. I don't need a hall pass either. I have three sexy men."

"I still can't believe the age difference doesn't bother you," Elaine says, sighing, letting her head fall back over the edge of the jacuzzi. "Then again, if it means you can do things like this, sign me up."

We all laugh. Sophia shrugs. "When you love someone, age doesn't matter. It's the connection that's important. I wouldn't be my best self without my husbands. We add something to each other's life. It's more than love, it's ..."

She shrugs and smiles. "When I find the word for it, I'll let you know."

"Massimo is still ..." Danny tries to look passive, but the corner of her mouth lifts. "He's annoying, but he's my favorite person in the world. I can't imagine not telling him about my day every day or listening to his stories and ideas. Not to mention ...

he's such a devoted father. He gets so upset when Gio chooses me over him."

We all laugh. Elaine pouts. "I feel like the odd one out. I'm the only one who's not married or with someone. I thought I'd be before Valerie."

"Are you saying I'm unlovable?" I ask, surprised.

"No, you just never showed an interest in relationships. I tried to push guys at you that were crushing on you and you ignored them or ended up becoming friends even though they were into you," she huffs.

"I did not know," I say.

Of course, I get teased for that all day. While the girls take a break, I go to the venue to verify that everything is going okay. I take care of a few issues, then run into the last person I expected–my mother. She looks around at everything, then looks at me.

Her eyes widen, and I narrow mine. "Sightseeing?"

"Valerie, I'd like you to reconsider. I want to be here for you. So does your father."

I scoff, "the same man that accused my fiancés of holding me hostage?"

"He's better now. Just call him. He understands. He did plenty of research and-"

"Why do you want to be here?" I say, cutting through the bullshit. "You want to be here to object to my wedding? To complain about how I'm ruining the name of 'marriage'? Why, Mom?"

Her eyes water. "You're my only daughter and I want to be at your wedding. Just because I don't approve doesn't mean that I should be punished and miss this. If you keep me out, you're no better than your father."

I just stare at her. What the hell is she talking about? "What in the psychological warfare is this?"

"You're wrong," Chase says from behind me.

I turn to see him. He put a hand on my hip and I don't bother telling him we're not supposed to be around each other today. He squeezes my side. "Valerie is nothing like her father, and you are not welcome here. We only want to celebrate this day with people who support us, love us, and are happy for us."

"Thank you, baby boy," I whisper in his ear.

"You don't know our life. Valerie misremembers plenty and only sees the worst in people," my mother hisses. "Keeping me away from such a big moment-"

"Is something you should get used to," Chase uses the same tone he uses when addressing subordinates. "I won't allow anyone to leech onto my wife and I won't allow anyone to gaslight or sabotage her when she's worked so hard to be her own person."

"But-" My mom tries again.

"The answer is no. If you're lucky, we'll send you photos. However, Valerie has been in no contact with her father for long enough that he doesn't have a place in her life. I don't care about the home videos or the wonderful memories you have. I care about my wife's future. We've tried to include you and it's a toss up whether you'll be supportive," Chase says.

I tug on his shirt. I can't believe he's defending me, that he's being so firm and unwavering. I've gotten used to his playful, easy going side, but I can't remember the last time someone stood up to me with my mother. She pulls out the tears and I'm the terrible one–always.

On cue, she cries. "I've done so much for you! I tolerated so much. I'm working so hard to have a life with you, Valerie. Why are you letting this man treat me like this?"

"This man is going to be my husband as of tomorrow, and you can't even muster up his name?" I demand.

Her mouth opens and closes. She looks at Chase like she can come up with his name, but she says nothing. I nod. "Exactly. You want me in your life when it's convenient. You want to be there for the big moments to celebrate my achievements for yourself, but you don't get to be in those moments if you're not willing to *be* in my life."

"Valerie!" she sobs.

"Security has a note that you and your husband are not allowed here tomorrow. It will be enforced," I say.

Chase walks me inside to the stairs and I sit down, holding a hand to my chest. Chase lifts my chin. "Breathe like you tell your patients to, baby doll."

I do just that, squeezing his hand the whole time. Then, I speak. "What are you doing here?"

"I got a call about an issue with the kitchen set up. The caterer doesn't like it. I put my foot down," he says with a shrug. "I'm glad I was here."

"Me too," I say. "I can't believe she said that to me. I didn't even know what to say."

Chase sits beside me and kisses my temple while taking my hand in both of his. "You're nothing like your parents, Valerie. You strengthen the people around you. You are a good person and good for us."

"You're not second guessing marrying me, knowing what my family is like?" I ask. It's been on my mind. "I know Tristan is a breeze, but ..."

"All families are messy in some way or another. You've met our father and mother. Lief's parents are great together, but rarely in one place for long and are always rearranging their schedules," Chase says.

I nod once.

"And we're not marrying your family, baby doll. We're marrying you. None of us have second guesses. You already would have spotted them and knocked some sense into us," Chase promises. "No one reads us better than you."

There's no trace of deceit in his eyes. He holds my gaze as his eyes soften, then he pushes his hair out of his face. "Should I cut my hair before we get married?"

"Whatever you want, Chase." I move closer and kiss him. "I love you. If you want to, do it. I want you as the man you are ... but that doesn't go for Lief. I'd be so sad."

He laughs and rubs my back, hugging me. "What do you mean? I didn't see you today."

"Of course not," I murmur.

"We got here at separate times and your mom wasn't here," he whispers. "Tomorrow, we're walking down the aisle, saying a ton of sappy things and we're going to compete to make you cry, then we're going to take turns stealing you from the reception and from photos to start the honeymoon early."

"Well, now that I know, I'll have to give Kon more jobs," I tease.

He rubs my hands and squeezes them tight. "I can't wait to see you in your dress. Can't wait to hear you say, I do, and can't wait to hear you call me your husband."

"I can't call you baby boy anymore can I? You're a boss now," I hum.

"You better not change nicknames on me now." He winks and stands. He stretches and sighs. "Are you determined to have this night apart?"

"It's not easy for me either," I murmur. "It's not, but I want tomorrow to be special in every way. Let me stay with the girls and you guys stay together making a long to-do list for our honeymoon."

"Can do, baby doll," he promises, offering me his hand.

I hop up with him and we part ways without a kiss. It doesn't matter though. Seeing Chase, feeling his support, knowing that we're going into this wedding knowing all of each other's worst secrets, makes everything feel right.

Now I just have to finish my vows for Lief since I'm not as good with words as he is and hope that Sophia finished her maid of honor speech.

"Everything will be fine," I tell myself.

SEVENTEEN

Lief

"Where the hell is my tux?" Hunter yells.

"What do you mean, the flowers are delayed?" Chase bellows into his phone.

I watch them try to tackle each issue the morning of our wedding day. I sigh, grab a phone, and call my father. "Can you bring the backup flowers please and a tux in Hunter's size? I think we'll also need some food."

"Fucking fix it!" Chase orders.

"Sounds like you might need more than food," my father says.

"I'll call my bride for some sedatives," I say.

"We'll meet you at the venue and get everything taken care of. Don't worry," he says before hanging up.

It's not a challenge. I rarely worry about anything. I just fix it or find an alternate option. Hunter hangs up and counts ten deep breaths, just like Valerie taught him. He looks at me. "Where's your issue?"

"I'm having a tux brought for you and my father has back up flowers. They're fake versions of what we purchased. I have insurance on all our deposits in case someone doesn't come through. The cake is being delivered in an hour," I say.

Chase hangs up and rubs his temple. "I went to the venue yesterday, I did all these checks, and I was told everything was on schedule. We can't let Valerie know."

"Why? Is she having problems? Did you see her yesterday? I only got a text this morning," Hunter says, pulling out his phone.

I stand and take his phone, pointing at him with it. "Valerie is fine. No matter what happens, we are going down that aisle, remember?"

"How dare you not be stressed," he growls, snatching his phone back.

I shrug. "Stressing about this won't help the situation, it will only make it harder to work through."

"Says the guy our wife uses as an experiment," Chase barks.

I touch the braid that's still in my hair from yesterday. I made sure it would stay, slept carefully. If I had my way, she would have done more, but I'll keep this reminder of Valerie.

It's a miracle we make it out of the house an hour later. Already, I've had to give orders to verify people with the guest list and to keep out press.

Chase had to make it clear it's a private wedding since somehow the date got leaked.

"Just wait until we get there," Hunter sighs as he drives. "We'll be fine, Chase. Lief will have to deal with the over eager venue manager. She's got a thing for you, Lief."

"Valerie took care of that with a threat," I reply.

"Oh yeah, because that's going to stop someone when they want you," Chase snorts.

"I appreciate the compliment," I reply.

"Can you muster some kind of emotion for us? This is supposed to be the happiest day of our lives and we're up here stressed while you're just the picture of peace," Hunter says while glowering at me in the rearview.

My lips split into a huge smile. "We're marrying Valerie today. Every plan could fall apart as long as we get to marry her. Nothing else matters. I'm overjoyed."

"Wow, a big smile like that proves it," Chase murmurs.

"Nothing else matters," I say again.

When we get to the venue, and into our room, I see Roman show up. Hunter turns to look at him. "What other problems are there?"

"The bride is concerned one of you three will sneak out to see her. I'm here to keep that from happening," he reports.

Hunter shoots him a glare. I know he was planning just that. How can I lie when I was hoping to do the same thing?

"Valerie is fine. The dress and everything else is right where it should be," Roman assures us. "The photographer's going to come in to take pictures of you three getting ready."

"Good luck, I don't have a-"

Hunter stops talking when he sees a bag on a hanger with his name on it. He opens it and sees an expensive tux in his size. He looks at me and I shrug. "My parents are capable."

"Remind me to get them an amazing Christmas present," he mumbles.

We take our time getting ready, but pose for photos as requested. Hunter does some photos in the hallway with the gold lining and in the library. Chase takes some photos on the stairs and against a gorgeous window on the landing. I let the photographer choose for me. I'm placed in the room with murals. I pose, then the three of us joke around and relax with some vodka.

Mr. Volkov joins us after a moment. Hunter and Chase are both on edge with parents right now, but Mr. Volkov approaches me. "I hope you protect your wife the same way you've protected my sons all these years. She's lucky to have all three of you."

He hands me a dagger. "Tradition."

I shrug and put it in my coat. As if I don't have a knife on me. I know our wife will. I look over at

Lev as he whistles at us before joining. "I feel under-dressed."

"Good," Hunter chuckles before patting his chest.

Gunner joins as well and winks at us. "I have a message for you."

"From our bride?" Chase asks, focused on our woman.

"From Konstantin. He's running security and wanted to let you know there have been no problems," Gunner salutes us.

I shake my head. "Kon would never allow the two problems to get in."

"Two?" Mr. Volkov asks.

Chase's face darkens. "Valerie's parents are unwelcome. I won't have anyone insulting my wife."

Hunter pats his back in agreement.

"Things can be done about that," Mr. Volkov argues.

"It's worse that they know she's living away from them and they don't get to have any part in her life," Hunter says. "Is Vanya here?"

"Yes," Mr. Volkov smiles. "She is. She's not expecting anything, Hunter."

"I hope she's ready to dance," he murmurs. "She deserves a dance on her sons' wedding day."

"At least one," Chase says with a smile.

"Your parents, Lief?" Mr. Volkov asks.

"They've been helping with some last-minute tasks. They'll be in the audience," I report.

Mr. Volkov shakes all our hands. "If any woman was to be involved in our business at a high rank, it's Valerie. She's a good woman."

None of us point out it's the nicest thing he's ever said about her. We take a few more photos, but I can tell we're getting antsy.

My phone buzzes and the guys glare at me. They left their phones upstairs. I put it on speaker. "Hello, pet."

"I'm dying for food. These snacks aren't doing anything!" she complains. "Please tell me I'm not the only one that's hungry. How are you? Chase? Hunter?"

"We're good, Dorogaya," Hunter assures her. "Are you stressed?"

"Not even a little." I can hear the smile in her voice. "I'm impatient to get down the aisle with you three. We made it here and nothing can stop us now."

"It could rain. What if things are missing? What if the D. J. messes up or-" Chase lists all the things that could go wrong.

"None of that is important," she says with a sigh. "You three are. You're here. You're uninjured. We made it."

"Get off the phone! You can't order a pizza for your own wedding!" Sophia says in the background.

"She can do what she wants. She's the bride!" Danny argues. "Oh, Gio, hi baby."

I roll my eyes. "We love you, pet."

"So much, baby doll," Chase agrees.

"Can we start this wedding early so we can get to the fun?" Hunter asks.

She laughs. "Let the photographers do their job. Then we'll have our photos together with the wedding party and the reception. I miss all three of you."

We drag out the call until someone takes Valerie's phone and hangs up. I can't wait to have her in my arms again. Last night was the worst night of sleep I've had in months. I miss having her. I can see the guys feel the same.

Chase looks at his watch as we have another round of drinks. "Twenty minutes to go."

"Twenty minutes is too long. We can just walk out early," Hunter grumbles.

"It's not just our day," I remind them. "It's for our family and friends, too. Let them get all the talking out so there aren't any interruptions during the ceremony."

Lev joins again and some of the other impor-tant people come in. They shake Chase's hands, promise him wonderful presents, and do the same to Hunter. I'm ignored until Chase points at me. "We have a third man getting married. A devoted man. He deserves just as much happiness."

I blink in surprise. I'm used to being in the corner, not the spotlight. I shake hands anyway. Before we can order food of our own, it's time to walk out. Mr. Volkov walks out with Vanya on his arm as the music softens. My parents go next, both looking back at me with huge smiles. The officiant follows, then Chase walks out.

A few people clap. Hunter walks out next. His pace is too fast, but no one points it out. I take my place at the end of the line. It's the order we'll marry her in, but it seems silly for Valerie to be running up and down the aisle. We had to make some changes to account for all the differences.

Danny and Gunner come down the aisle and I'm sure Gunner is cracking jokes to keep that smile on Danny's face the whole time. Elaine walks down the aisle with Roman. She's smiling and tearing up already. She takes a few breaths as she stands with Danny.

"You guys are not ready for your bride," Gunner hisses at us with a knowing smile. "Even Sophia's crying."

"She's pregnant, that doesn't count," Hunter says. "Her hormones are getting to her."

"Sure, we'll see," Roman says with a smile.

Sophia and Lev walk down. Lev got the 'best man' position as a political move for Chase, but he looks good next to Sophia. Of course, Sophia keeps dabbing at her eyes. She smiles, but her emotions are getting to her.

She walks up and stands in front of Danny. They whisper, and I worry for a moment about Valerie. Is she having second thoughts? Is she upset her parents aren't here? Has someone tried to take her from us again?

Nick carries Link out with the rings and then the music shifts again. There's no going back as Valerie's song plays.

I glance over at the audience and spot Tristan. My brow furrows. "Wasn't Tristan walking her down the aisle?"

"No one can give Valerie away but Valerie," Hunter murmurs with adoration.

He's not wrong. Valerie's always done as she pleased, even if we told her not to, even if it was life and death. Our wedding isn't any different and it shouldn't be. She deserves to be in control the way she wants to be.

I adjust, sure I will not handle this. Chase takes a slow breath, preparing himself. I nudge Hunter. "You wrote your vows, right?"

"Shit, they're in our changing room," he curses.

I pat his shoulder. "You know what you feel, Hunter. You'll get it right."

He nods, but then our eyes are focused on our bride as she appears. Gorgeous, alone, powerful and sexy. I don't stand a chance of getting through this wedding without crying.

EIGHTEEN

Valerie

AFTER ANOTHER DEEP BREATH, I TAKE MY FIRST
step down the aisle. I hate everyone is standing and
staring at me, but I push my shoulders back and
walk down the aisle with my dress trailing behind
me. The veil doesn't cover my face. I didn't want it
to. I wanted to see my grooms.

Chase's cheeks go pink, then his eyes water as
he smiles. Hunter bites his fist, but I see the huge
grin he's trying to hide and the love in his eyes. Lief
is staring, his lips parted, eyes all warm as his face
turns red.

My own eyes water and I look up so I don't cry,
but a laugh escapes before I get to the altar. How
can I stay calm when my men are looking at me like
they've never seen anything more beautiful in their
life?

I take a few breaths as I reach the front and pass

my flowers to Sophia. She's all out crying now. I touch her face and sniff. "If you cry, I'm going to cry."

A few people laugh, but then I turn to see my men. Their matching gold ties, the purple orchids in their pockets, the suits themselves are all great, but their faces make my heart beat double time. They're just so ... normal and I love it. I love they love me, that they can't stop staring.

The officiant starts everything off, but makes it quick, quoting a poetry passage that we all agreed on. Then it gets to the part for the vows. We decided we'd all do our vows, then do everything else as a group.

God, I'm not ready. Who knows what's going to come out of their mouths? I just know I'm going to end up crying because it's them.

"Chase, you wrote your own vows, is that correct?" the officiant asks.

He nods and reaches in his suit. He fumbles from one pocket to the other before pulling out his piece of paper. Taking a slow breath, he shakes his head before looking at me again and taking my hand, pulling me a step closer.

"You are too far away, baby doll," he whispers.

I laugh and squeeze his hand. "I know."

He's passed a microphone and rolls his eyes, but adjusts so he can read his vows and hold the mic, since letting go of me is not an option. "Valerie, I think the fact that we broke the rules two nights ago because none of us could sleep apart says plenty. You are a dream come true. I've never met anyone as supportive, open, compassionate, yet cut-throat as you. We've been through so much and each adventure, problem, and quiet moment at home has brought you deeper into my heart."

And I just lost the battle with my tears. One runs down my cheek and I sniff.

"Thanks to you, I can admit there's plenty I don't know, but you're the partner I want when I'm taking all that uncertainty on. I want you by my side through all of it. No matter how bad it gets, or how wonderful it gets, I know that having you ... that's all I need to be happy. I vow to always make the little moments count, even if that means taking twice as long to make the bed. I vow to protect you, to support you, and most important, to love you the way you deserve to be loved. I'll love you by being your rock in every storm. I'll love you by making everything that's boring fun. I'll love you by never letting you question, forget, or wonder how I feel about you forever."

I take a few minutes and wipe my eyes before he passes me the microphone. Chase is already tearing up, too.

I mouth I love him, then clear my throat. I tried to memorize what I wrote. That was half my morning since I knew I'd get things messed up if I tried to bring out my vows with me. "Chase, you've grown so much since we met. You were a quiet workaholic that I connected with because we're both ambitious and don't like to stop when there are still things to do. But seeing your silly side, seeing you enjoy life's little moments with a huge smile and a silly dance or comment ... that's when I fell in love with you. You're so careful, so loving, always put others first, and never want to miss a moment where you can help. I'm so lucky that you refused to let me go, that you stayed, that you *never* let me think myself out of what I want."

My voice breaks and I have to collect myself before I continue. He nods to me, eyes all teary and his cheeks red.

"I vow to always correct you when you're wrong." Some people laugh at that, but Chase nods. I smile. "I vow to make time for us every week–just for us. I vow to interrupt you when you work from home, to always embarrass you by supporting your silly side, and to let you spoil me. And I vow to always remind you how much I love you as you are, for who you are, not what you do or your last name. I can't wait to be your wife and to take on the world together."

Chase groans and wipes his eyes. "You're too good for me, baby doll."

"Not even close, baby boy," I say, just as close to crying as he is.

I fan my face and hand the microphone back to

the officiant. "Hunter Volkov, do you have your vows?"

"I have plenty," he says, smiles a happy, boyish smile that makes my heart beat unsteadily. He glances to the officiant.

He takes a slow breath. "I'm not that great at being serious with you, Valerie, because you make it so easy to be more. I smile with you, laugh with you, annoy you and ruffle your feathers, challenge you, adore you, and admire you. I can't get enough of you. It took work for us to get here and ..." his brow furrows before he slows down. "And I don't regret that for a second. That work has made us both better people and made our relationship so much stronger. I will spend the rest of my life reminding you why you chose me and to prove that it was a good choice, Dorogaya."

He squeezes my hand nearly to the point of pain. "Even when we fight, I promise to love you. I promise to bore you with history facts. I promise–I swear, I will never let you have a boring week. I'll give you plenty of reasons to stick to forty hours a week. And I promise that you are the only woman that will ever have my heart. You have become such a huge part of me in such a short time that I can't wait to see where we are in five years, or ten, or when I'm old and forgetful and get to fall in love with you all over again. You're more than the woman I love. You're my soul mate and I will *never* take that for granted."

I shake my head and have to pull my hand from his to get my tears under control. Hunter pulls out a handkerchief and wipes my eyes. "I will only make you cry for good reasons."

We put ourselves back together and I fan my face before taking the microphone and Hunter's hand. "Hunter, you are a whirlwind of a person. You're wild, spontaneous, hotheaded, and intense."

He cocks his head to the side.

"And I fu- I love that about you. I've never met someone who feels everything so intensely and doesn't hide it. I love that you're so genuine. Even if you annoy me, even if you drive me up the wall, I always feel *something* and I always feel lucky that you're mine," I say.

He looks up, trying not to cry, and motions for me to continue. I smile. "You're a closet nerd, you've made me love Indiana Jones, and you never forget any small detail I tell you. You remind me how good it is to just let go and enjoy life and seeing you become such an amazing man when you already started out so strong is.. staggering. I promise to always work with you and not against you. I promise to join in on your hobbies and try everything you're interested in. I vow to never make you feel second best or forgotten because you're so damn important to me that I learned Russian for you."

He lets out a soft sound, and I realize he's

crying. He's also close to breaking my fingers since he's holding me so tight.

"At your best and worst, I'm on your side and love you all the same. You are the man I never knew I needed and now, I just can't let you go, even when I tried," I laugh once. "I love your outlook and the way you want to improve the world, and I'm so ready to be there when you do with the perks of a new title."

"Fuck, Valerie, I hate that I can't kiss you," he says in Russian, making a few people laugh.

"Easy, Krolik, soon," I promise with a wink. He shakes his head and steps back, taking care of his eyes.

"Finally, Lief Prins. Did you write your own vows or-" the officiant asks.

"I know what I'm going to say," Lief says.

His bottom lip trembles, and I take a step forward. He holds my hand, then laces our fingers together. "Valerie, I love you. That's all I needed to know to marry you. I don't love easy and I don't always show what I feel, but you always know. You're the first person to ever want to take care of me, to see me as more than some muscle that stands in a corner and is handy in a fight. There has never been and will never be anyone who compares to you. I could live a thousand years and that would still be true."

My lips part as a little sob leaves my throat.

Lief rubs my hand with his thumb. "I will

always cook with you and for you. I will always tell you what the weather is going to be. I'll spar with you and never let you win. I will always ask for you to braid my hair. Beyond all of that, I will love you every single day as easily as I breathe. Whatever you want, you only have to ask, and I will make it a reality. You're the woman I never thought I'd meet, and calling you my wife is the best thing I could ever do."

He hands the microphone to me, as if he didn't just ruin my makeup in one go. I notice the braid in his hair and almost lose myself all over again.

"Lief, I love you. I love your soft side. I love your intense side. Love our conversations, even if other people don't get them, and I always learn something new when we're together. I don't care if other people don't understand you, if they lust after you, if they challenge you because I know you, I trust you, and I love you. I promise to never let either of us stay mad at each other. I promise never to hold back when I have questions or feelings. Promise that you will never regret *almost* retiring because I will fill every single moment, even if we just sit and talk or try new things together."

He smiles, and I step back, looking at my men. "I didn't think I'd ever get married. I thought love was something in movies and books and a word people threw around too freely, but you three ... you're the only people I could ever marry, the only men I could ever love and I can't wait to have all of you forever."

We trade rings and the officiant barely gets out his questions before we're saying, "I do". I kiss each of my men, savoring the moment, and let go of my control, crying as they hug me and tell me again how much they love me.

We did it. We made it.

NINETEEN

Hunter
_____

SHE'S OURS. VALERIE IS FINALLY OURS. PEOPLE cheer, but I don't care. I pull her from Chase and Lief to kiss her, gripping the back of her neck as I suck and lick her tongue. She draws back and touches my face.

"Your vows were beautiful, Hunt," she whispers before kissing me again. "I love you."

"Last night was impossible," Chase groans as he kisses her. "Never again."

Lief nods and strokes her cheek. "We have photos to take and a reception to get started. Let's walk down the aisle."

"And you and I have a paper to sign, Lief," Valerie reminds him.

She holds my hand and Chase's hand while Lief keeps a hand on her back as we walk down the aisle to cheering and clapping. We take pictures together: serious ones, romantic ones, and silly ones.

Then she gets pictures with us individually. I pull her close, my arm around her waist as I stare into her gorgeous eyes. From my peripheral, I notice someone adjusting her skirt, but I keep stroking her cheek until our foreheads touch.

"I love you," she whispers, her nose rubbing against mine. "So much, Hunt. You have no idea how much."

A few pictures are taken, but I love the fact her dress is sleeveless. I bend down and kiss across her shoulder, her neck, then her mouth. She slides her hand into my hair and kisses me back with so much passion I almost pass out. I love it. I love how desperate she is for me.

Valerie pulls away and giggles as I grin. I twirl her under my arms and cross her arms across her abdomen. She looks up at me, eyes all big and eager as she pants.

"Hold it!" the photographer orders.

Her gaze sizzles through me, and it takes everything in me to keep from kissing her. Valerie's lips part as she stares at me. "Krolik."

Just that word breaks me. I kiss her again, devouring her mouth and pressing her against the wall. She already took photos with the other guys and now she's mine. The photographer tries to get Valerie and me in order as I move her toward the stairs. But Valerie isn't listening anymore than I am. She giggles as she bundles her dress up in one hand and takes my hand, following where I lead.

I hear more cameras flicker, then I growl out. "Photos are done. Start the reception."

Valerie laughs as I pick her up. She kisses across my neck, teasing me with light flicks of her tongue until I find a room. I shut the door and see Valerie backing away from me.

"How sweet of you, Hunter. This is where my reception dress is," Valerie purrs.

I arch an eyebrow. "Lucky me. You'll have something to wear when I tear that dress off you."

She puts her palm against my chest. "I didn't say you get to have me or tear my very expensive dress. I like it. I want to keep it."

"I'll replace it," I say, pulling her closer to me.

She smirks. "Hunter Volkov, when was the last time I made you work for me?"

"Not today," I growl. "After the small amount of time we got yesterday, not having you in bed with me last night, do you think I'll let you get away?"

She smiles and reaches behind her, undoing something. Her dress loosens on her and she takes another step back and another until she stops at the window. "What was it you said I had to do to get a kiss or your touch at that gala so long ago? Or after?"

"Oh, you're going to beg for it. That's for sure," I promise.

She lets her gown fall to the floor, pooling around her feet. It reveals lingerie that makes me want to take back my comment. I'm ready to beg my wife. The white lace corset, the silk white panties. I lean in closer and notice something on the top of her panties.

She snaps them against her hip.

Hunter. Chase. Lief. I groan and close the space between us, pressing my hand on the walls so I don't touch her. "Dorogaya, you tease me too much."

"Do I?"

I nod and lean in closer. She pulls at my jacket. I pull it off, toss it to the side, then free myself of the suspenders. Valerie licks her bottom lip as I undo one button at a time, freeing myself from the shirt.

Valerie lets out a soft moan and reaches for the top clasp on her corset. She undoes it, then another until I grab her hands and pin them above her head. "Use your words to tell me what you want, Dorogaya. Beg."

"You want me as much as I want you, Krolik," she croons. "Why should I beg?"

"Because I can edge you and make you feel things. I don't care about the reception. I don't care about showing up," I say, my lips brushing hers in an almost kiss. "All I want is to claim my wife as mine."

She lets out a soft breath. "Hunter ..."

"There is nothing in this entire world that is as important to me as you. Kissing you, touching you, keeping you safe, knowing you're smiling because of me, calling you mine ... that's what matters."

"Kiss me," she whispers.

"That sounded like a demand. You know what it means to beg. You've begged me before," I tsk.

"Please," she whimpers. "Kiss me like you wanted to when I said, I do. Fuck me so hard, so that everyone downstairs hears. Make me your wife in the way that matters. Please, Krolik. Please, I need you."

I give in, kissing her like I need her to survive. I undo her corset in record time just so I can kiss her skin, feel her nails on my back, digging into my shoulders as she pants and moans. I suck her nipple hard, then bite, unable to restrain myself.

Mine, Valerie, is mine. I rip her panties as I drag them down her legs, then push my fingers into her pussy. Her head arches back and Russian drags from her throat. "Fuck me like I'm yours, Hunter."

I groan and kiss her hard and deep as she fumbles with my pants before getting them off. We don't need a bed. We only need each other. I prove that by freeing her of my fingers right before she can come.

"Hunter, please! Please, I need your cock buried inside me. I want to come with you!" she begs.

"I live to please you, Dorogaya," I answcr as I thrust into her hard. Her leg wraps around my hip as I fuck her against the window. "Shame we can't have photographers get this on camera."

"They're not allowed to see you come. Not allowed to see the faces you make when I'm inside you," I snarl before grabbing her breast hard. I fuck her hard, relentlessly, trying to prove she's mine, to convince us both this is forever, not a marriage that's going to end.

"Yes, Hunt!" she yells before biting my neck and tightening her hold on me.

I grip her thigh harder, then cup her ass against me as we move together. Valerie is everything. Her perfume filling my nose, her warm body pressed to mine, the way her pussy clenches me tighter, like she can pull me in deeper. All of it is a heaven I'll live my life trying to deserve.

I grip her hair in my free hand and pull back so she has to look at me. "I fucking love you."

"I love you, Krolik! I love you so much. Oh, fuck ... yes, like that," she pants against my lips. "You .... yes!"

"Mine, Dorogaya. You're mine," I grunt against her mouth before kissing her again.

She digs her fingers into my hair and clutches my neck.

I'm already too close to the edge. I know it. She moans and her head falls back. "Hunt, yes! I'm so ..."

"Come for me. Don't you dare hold out," I order. "Come now!"

She yells my name as she comes, her legs squeezing me hard, forcing me deeper as I let go of my control. Pleasure sweeps through me, consuming me until all I see are stars. I hold her in place as my hips slow and still, her pussy clenching around me.

I groan and shake, stumbling back with her until we're on the bed. She giggles and strokes my chest while kissing me softly. "How did it feel to fuck me as my husband?"

I chuckle and look at the band around her finger with my engagement ring. I kiss her fingertip, then her rings. I press her palm to my cheek. "Sex with you is better than just about anything in the world."

Valerie smiles and kisses me again. "I love you, Krolik."

"I love you, Dorogaya," I reply while pressing my forehead to hers. I can feel her eyelashes against my skin and chuckle before kissing her again. "Alright, show me this fancy reception dress you have."

She jumps up, grabs her underwear and the corset, pulling both back on, then reaches into the closet. "I might need your help."

"Ah, seduce me, then put me to work. I see how it is," I tease.

I help her into the dress, kissing up her back just before I zip it. She looks at herself in the mirror. It still looks bridal. There's one strap that crosses her shoulder and the bodice has the same cut out style along the side, just like her wedding dress did. This one shows off her legs in the front, not even touching her knees as the fabric waves further and further down on the sides until the back. It reaches the ground with the same lace as her wedding dress, but doesn't touch the floor.

I kiss Valerie's neck. "It's beautiful, but everyone can see your garter and your knife."

She gasps and adjusts the knife, then the dress. It hangs perfectly, barely covering the garter, but doing its job all the same.

She turns and pushes against my chest. "Come on, we're already late."

"I had to have you before Lief or Chase. Chase gets to parade you around as his mafia goddess, Lief gets you on paper..." I trail off, not wanting to sound ungrateful.

"And you get me dressing up in all those costumes to make studying history more fun. You get me to read to. You get me to train in the gym, you get me as your wife," she says.

I kiss her again. How can Valerie make me feel so complete, even though I'm sharing her?

I don't bother overthinking it as she leads us to the closed doors of the reception area outside. Lief and Chase are waiting. Lief looks at his nails before peeking up at Valerie. Chase huffs. "About time. You're losing your touch, Hunter. You used to be faster than that."

"Trust me, you both are going to struggle to keep your sanity when you see what else our wife has for us," I say, loving that I can call her my wife — our wife. I kiss the top of her head and fix her hair. Chase adjusts her makeup, putting her back together. Lief shakes his head. "Couldn't even fuck her without ruining her hair and makeup."

"Hey, I did plenty of the fucking ... and seducing," Valerie says. "And I believe I was told that we weren't leaving until each of you had fucked me. One down."

"We didn't say just once," I whisper in her ear.

She giggles and shakes her head. "All three of you–from so romantic I'm crying, to horndogs in less than an hour."

"You better get used to it, baby doll. This is your forever," Chase says. "Now, Hunter got to have you and Lief and you are about to sign a paper, so I get to walk in with you."

I roll my eyes. We may marry her together, but I have a feeling we're always going to be fighting over her.

TWENTY

Valerie

CHASE AND I WALK IN. THEN IT'S A WHIRLWIND OF action. Everyone wants to say hello, food is served and we almost miss it, but Kon refuses to let anyone take our plates away. He nods when we sit down. I take his hand. "Kon, go be with your girlfriend. I'm sure she's eager for your attention."

"I.. I was given a job, Valerie," he says. "I need to check with security and-"

"Eat, Kon. Tell security to do their job and sit with Julianna for a bit," I insist. I arch an eyebrow when he refuses, letting my features harden. "Are you going to tell a bride no on her wedding day?"

"N-no, of course not. Never, Mrs ..."

"Prins," Lief takes my hand. "Valerie Prins."

"Right, right," he hurries away.

Lief touches his ear and I lean back. "That better not be a com in your ear. In fact, I *know* it's not, because if it was, I'd have to tug that braid out of your hair. It's our wedding day!"

He hands me the com so I can hear the security guys. "Lief's a softy now. Married and smiling for everyone. Can you believe we used to be afraid of him?"

Another guy speaks up. "Say what you want about him. Valerie is terrifying, married or not. I bet she has multiple weapons on her right now."

"I could take her, or convince her she doesn't want to fight," another says.

I arch an eyebrow at Lief. He nods once. "I'm making a list of who I'm going to fire. Dmitri just made number one."

"Oh please, Valerie has the Volkov brothers and Lief. You wouldn't know what to do with her, not the other way around," another guy says.

"She'd castrate all of you for talking about her or her men just like that," a cool, calm voice says. "In fact, I'd be careful if I were you. Plenty of loyal and smart people are on this frequency. I'd be surprised if Kon or Lief himself aren't listening."

All chatter ceases, and Lief smiles before pulling it out and setting it on the table. "Lev will keep them in line."

"Good, because it's time for the mother-son dances." I pat his leg. "Guess who's up first?"

"Chase," he says.

Chase gets up and takes Vanya's hand. They dance together and Chase is smiling while Vanya's fighting her tears. At least I'm not the only one who cried today. Hunter takes a slow breath, kisses my cheek, and whispers in my ear.

"I want to keep being a better man for you, Valerie. You're going to have two wonderful mothers-in-law, so you'll never have to feel alone," Hunter promises.

I stare after him as he goes to dance with Vanya as well. I squeeze Lief's hand. "When are you three going to stop making me fall in love on a daily basis?"

"When we get you to fall in love on an hourly basis," he answers.

"Is the weather going to stay this nice?" I ask, leaning toward him. "All through the reception?"

"All through the reception," he promises, kissing my temple. "The rain will wait until tomorrow, just for us."

"You keep being right. I'll assume that you control the weather, Viking."

"I'd be willing to try for you, Viper," he answers.

I kiss him, touching the braid I put in his hair. He draws back and takes my hand. "I did something for you."

"What? Lief, the grooms don't get the bride a present. You are my present, and I'm yours," I say.

He almost says something, but Josefine walks up. "The ceremony was so beautiful. I cried with what you said, Lief. You've never shared your feelings like that before."

"Valerie means the world to me. I don't want her ever thinking it's one-sided," he answers.

"I never do, Viking. You always make me feel loved," I say. "Now go dance with your mother."

Lief goes and dances with his mother. I grin at them as Hunter sits beside me again. "Are you sure you don't want to dance with Tristan or ... Roman? He could be a father figure."

I laugh. "Absolutely not. My next dance belongs to Chase, then you, then Lief. I don't know what you three have planned."

"Well, we took dance lessons, at least Chase and I did. Lief might have on his own time, but I can't say for sure," Hunter sighs.

Before I know it, we're up. Chase holds my hand and leads me in a simple waltz, then more, something close and intense, like a tango. I giggle as he spins me, then catches me against his body. I kiss him. "I love you, baby boy."

"I love you. I meant everything I said at the altar. You will never have a chance to think any of us don't love you, because we do. You're everything to us," Chase says, promising me.

"You can't say that when you have an entire business to run." I kiss his neck. "It's okay. I like that we have other things that are important to us and we're not codependent."

Chase dips me back, then pulls me up, again

cradling me far closer than anyone would say is appropriate. He kisses my neck. "I'm going to steal you. You know that, right?"

"If you tell me, it's not stealing," I whisper back.

He spins me out and Hunter catches me. He presses his lips to my temple and doesn't even pretend to be sly about how he's dancing. I love it. I love how silly he is, I love how much fun he has, love that I can forget the world in his arms as we laugh and tease one another. He lifts me and I gasp before he pulls me back down his body, eyes serious.

Our faces brush and my heart lodges in my throat. Hunter brushes my hair from my face and runs his nose over my temple to whisper in my ear. "I liked you better in less."

"You always do," I pant. "Imagine our honeymoon."

He groans. "You're not packing anything at all. It wouldn't make sense. You're going to spend more time naked than not."

"So dirty." I bite his bottom lip. "This is supposed to be a romantic dance."

"Romance always leads to sex. I just like to skip parts," Hunter says. "But I know you like a little tease. Should I take off my shirt again?"

I pull him by his shirt. "Absolutely not. Woo me, Hunter."

"I will soon enough," he promises.

"Soon?" I ask. "Do you have to study?"

"No. I'll get a book and read you fun history

facts until you're so horny and in love with me, you can't help yourself," he teases.

He disappears before I can follow up on that, and Lief offers me his hand. I take it and he sweeps me up into a simple waltz, but then the music moves faster. He spins me until I gasp and pulls me close. "Fuck, Lief."

"Just let me lead you. You can trust me," he whispers.

I exhale and nod. It's fast and wild, some kind of swing with other elements until the music slows again and he pulls me back into his arms. I stroke over those arms. "What is this present you mentioned?"

"Less of a present and more of ... a sign," Lief says.

"I want to see," I insist.

"It's not appropriate to show you ... yet," he says, his blue eyes threatening to ruin my sanity.

"Lief," I whisper.

"You have my heart forever and I want to prove it to you and anyone else who ever sees me shirtless," he says.

I realize I've stopped dancing at that point. I'm just panting, staring at my husband. "Get me off the dance floor."

His eyes soften. "Are you going to be sick, pet?"

"Sure, that's what it is." I take his hand and lead him from the dance floor. The second I find a secluded spot, I pull his tie, dragging him down to kiss me. Lief groans and lets me back him against the wall.

"I'm not patient," I say against his lips. "I don't want to wait to see it. Now."

He nods, glances around, then pulls me between two brick walls. I push Lief down and he chuckles before taking off his jacket and setting it to the side. I rip through his shirt, not caring about the buttons. Lief looks down, then at the knife in my hand, the same one he gave me.

"I never go anywhere without it, Lief. It's the best thing I've ever been given, other than the rings on my fingers," I whisper.

Lief looks from me to the knife, then pulls it from my hand, setting it down on the ground as he kisses me. He rolls on top of me and bunches my dress up. Before he can push my underwear to the side, I grab his hand. "Look first, Viking. It's my present."

He looks down, sees his name on my panties, then cups my face in his hand as he kisses me, his tongue plundering deep, but there's something so soft, so warm, so perfect. I stroke over his chest and he hisses, drawing back. I look down and see a viper there, in gray and black, right in the center of his chest. I kiss just above it and look up at him.

"You got ... me?" I ask.

He nods and leans forward, kissing my fore-head. He kisses me again and again, deeper and hungrier, before pushing my underwear off to the side as I drag his pants down. He thrusts into me and I gasp, arching back and moaning.

Lief covers my mouth. "Be quiet or we'll get caught."

"I don't care. The knife is right there," he says against my lips.

I dig my fingers into his ass and kiss across his collarbone. "That feels so good."

"You feel good," he argues.

I drag my nails down the back of his neck, kissing him deeper as he fucks me, taking his time and making sure I feel everything. I shake my head at him, then bite his bottom lip. "Fuck me. Really fuck me."

Lief groans and bundles me in his arms, pulling me onto his lap. I ride him hard and fast, pulling his hair, kissing him, ruining his clothes the best way I can as we try to stay quiet. We cover each other's mouths as we get close, and I whine against his palm. Lief pumps his hips up and into me over and over again until my eyes roll back. He grabs the back of my neck, so I stay right where I am as I come.

Lief's hips lift, then he pulls out of me. I wrap my lips around his cock. Lief groans and thrusts deep in my throat before he comes apart. He bites his hand to stay quiet as his back arches and he grinds into my mouth. I draw back and swallow, licking my lips.

"Fuck," he pants.

"You should show Hunter what it means to be romantic," I pant.

Lief helps put me back together, then lifts me up. He can't fix his shirt, so he just buttons his jacket over himself before sliding my knife into the side of my underwear. He grins and pulls me close. "Never stop being the woman I married."

TWENTY-ONE

Chase

I ROLL MY EYES AS PEOPLE DANCE AND IGNORE THE fact that Valerie and Lief have been gone for a while. I nudge Hunter. "Think we're the only ones who have noticed?"

Lev and a few others chuckle, and I shake my head. "Unlikely."

"Are you upset she didn't run off with you?"

I turn to give him shit, but I see how serious he is. Hunter leans closer. "She loves you, Chase. I feel like I can't compete with you. And you're worried about one upping us. You don't need to be. She loves us each differently, separately, perfectly."

I take a few slow breaths, then see Valerie leading Lief back. She wipes the corners of her mouth and assures Josefine that she's finc. Considering Lief's suit is done up, but not hiding the fact his buttons are useless, I'm sure they had plenty of fun.

Valerie comes back to us while Lief takes care of some security. She looks at me as she drinks some wine and strokes my face. "I miss you, Chase."

"I'm right here, baby doll," I promise, confused.

"It took every bit of control not to run to you last night," she whispers in my ear, taking my hand. "I love you, baby boy, and we haven't gotten enough time together."

I turn as she kisses my shoulder. Valerie peeks up at me and hides her smile. "Remember the yacht?"

"Which part? Should I be asking about the food, what happened in bed, what happened on deck ..." my hand slides over her knee.

She nods at me. "All of it, especially trying to be quiet while you touched me. So touch me, see if I can be good."

I can't resist. She pulls her dress up a bit to show her panties. Seeing my name there drives me crazy. I drop my fork and Valerie arches an eyebrow. "You better get that."

"Oh, I better?"

She pulls her panties to the side and spreads her legs. "You better, right now, or else."

I groan and drop to my knees. I spread Valerie's legs and devour her pussy while thrusting my fingers deep. She gasps and Hunter turns her chin to face him, kissing her, dragging out each flick of his tongue while motioning for me to hurry.

I lick and suck her clit, then try something new

with my tongue. Valerie's fingers grip my hair and she rocks her hips forward. I do it again and again, slipping my tongue around her clit, curling it, flattening it, trying a few different things until she comes for me. Hunter muffles her moan.

Grinning, I grab my fork and sit back up, licking my bottom lip and winking at Valerie.

She leans toward me and kisses me again and again. "How does your wife taste?"

I groan and pull her closer. "You are pulling at my nerves, woman."

"And now, let's get the bride and grooms on the dance floor. We need some dancing and a garter toss!"

We get swept up in the wedding. I see Kon sharing his woman before she takes a walk, then notice Sophia and Nick dancing close, having a good time without a care in the world.

I get to get Valerie's garter and stuff it in my pocket instead of tossing it. Everyone laughs. We cut the cake, go through the motions, do everything until people are drunk or on their way there. Even Hunter and Lief are having fun on the dance floor.

I pull Valerie tight and drag her away from the crowd, "now you're mine."

She nods and I drag her to a room I found earlier. She pants as she continues to kiss me, tasting like tequila and her. I shove her onto the bed and point at the dress. "Rip or save?"

"I love you," she moans. "Save."

I come down on top of her and unzip the back of her dress as we kiss. Instead of pulling it all the way down, I stop when it's below her breasts. I suck each nipple, lick and tease, just like I used my tongue on her under the table.

"Yes," she pants. "Oh, Chase ... Get this fucking dress off me."

I struggle and end up needing her help to get it off. She's in that damn little thong. I tear it. I don't care if she wants to keep it. I can't wait another second to have it. She grins down at me. "Have me, boss man."

Groaning, I climb on top of her while tearing off my shirt. She pulls at my buttons until she rips it over my head. "Chase, please, faster, more."

"So demanding. I thought I was the boss," I chuckle.

She grins and kisses me back, pulling me close. "You're naughty and I love it."

I tease her with my fingers as she teases me with hers, ripping my pants off the second she has a chance. I groan and chuckle. "Naughty girl."

"You should have stolen me first," she pants.

I slide into her. She's already so wet, already so perfect. Valerie gasps and strokes over my arms. "Chase.."

"I'm yours, baby doll," I moan into her mouth. "All yours. Forever. I'm not your boss." I thrust with each sentence. "Not your master. I'm yours."

Valerie gasps. "What ... what does that make me?"

I grin as I lick up her throat. I remember what she said on that damn recording. "You're a damn queen."

"Fuck, Chase!" She yells, clawing my back. I press her thighs to her body and pound into her harder and faster.

I'm so pent up, have wanted her even though we just had fun yesterday, not getting to see her, to touch her, to have her for even one night ruined me. I grab her hips, pull her closer and pound into her harder, taking everything I need.

Valerie comes apart, chanting my name, screaming for me. I groan and flip her over onto her knees. She nods. "Yes, please. Please."

She rocks back against me until I grab her hair and pull back. She whines and I kiss across her shoulders, the back of her neck, fucking her like we both need, then slowing down when that becomes too much.

She whines and arches her back. "Chase, please!"

I groan and jerk her back hard as I come, riding the high of the orgasm as she slumps under me. I collapse on top of her and laugh once. "How do you feel, wife?"

"Overwhelmingly satisfied, husband," she sighs. "How are you?"

BARBI COX

I roll her over and kiss her with a smile. "That one word makes me crazy."

"Better get used to it baby boy," she lifts her hand to show me her rings. "You're my husband forever and I don't want it any other way."

All I can do is stare at the woman who I now get to call my wife. I kiss her again and again. I don't want to leave. I don't have any plan to leave. I just keep kissing her, loving how she molds herself to me.

"Chase, I need more than one time with you," she pants.

"The party?"

"I married all three of you. I don't need a party. Lief and I signed the paperwork, we were seen at the reception, what's left but to live happily ever after?" Valerie draws a heart on my chest. "You're making me all soft and sappy."

The door opens and Hunter points. "There! Right there's my wife. Get her, Lief."

Lief pats Hunter's shoulder. "He's drunk."

"And stripping. My favorite version. Where's my poetry, Krolik?" Valerie asks.

"I am going to kiss you until I've outnumbered every damn star," he points at the ceiling. "And I am going to fuck you until you've had more orgasms than there are galaxies." He kicks out of his shoes. "And then I'm going to love you every minute of my existence."

Valerie blushes and I grin. Of course, he's

ridiculous when he's drunk, but she loves it. She loves *us* and that's all that matters. That's what's important.

Lief was right about that. Right before any of us were.

The three of us fuck and love our wife until she's so exhausted, she shakes her head when we touch her. She curls up between us and I stroke through her hair. Lief grins at me since Hunter's already passed out. "Can you get used to this life, boss?"

"I already am," I answer. "Now I need to find someone to replace me so I can retire in ten years and make the most of our life with our wife while we're still young."

Lief chuckles. I point at him. "You've smiled more today than I've ever seen you smile. And don't think I missed that new tattoo."

He rubs Valerie's hip and she hums in her sleep. He kisses her shoulder. "I have an excellent reason to keep smiling."

We fall asleep and take our time in the morning. Valerie joins us, still wearing white, but it's a simple, nice sundress. Hunter points at her. "Told you to pack nothing."

"That's for the honeymoon which starts tomorrow. How are my husbands?" She asks, absolutely glowing. The sun is going to have to work hard to outshine her.

And this is what we get forever. I want to pinch

myself. Hunter and Lief promise to take care of some things and Valerie joins me as I head home to get our things for the honeymoon together. She wraps herself around me as I remove things from the drier.

"What are you doing back there?" I ask.

She kisses across my skin. "Kissing each scar better. As your wife, I'm demanding that you don't get any new ones."

I turn in her arms. I want to promise her that, I want to promise her the world, but in our life, that's an impossible thing to offer. She touches my chest and shakes her head. "Lief stepped back from the front lines, but I want all my husbands all the time. I want every second we can have together. I don't want to see you or Hunter in the hospital again. I don't want to lose either of you."

"You won't," I promise. "We're survivors."

She sucks in a breath and looks up at me. Something hot and demanding and fierce, the same something I remember from when she was going to save Hunter from our aunt, fills her eyes. "If either of you die, I will be worse than any storybook dragon. Save the world from me, Chase."

I kiss her forehead. "I would fight death himself to stay right here with you. I'll stop killing, stop fighting myself, pick battles wisely. I will live for you, baby doll."

"That's a hell of a promise," Hunter says.

Valerie looks over at him. "You better promise

the same, Krolik. I just bound myself to all three of you and that means forever, as long as we live. That better be decades, centuries even."

He pulls her from me to kiss her. "I will become Frankenstein, replacing all my old worn out parts as long as it keeps you from threatening me with anything but fun."

She nods and looks at Lief.

He hesitates. "I can't promise what Chase did. I will kill for you, Valerie. I will fight for you. I will destroy anyone who touches you."

She keeps watching him. He sighs. "And I will win, as I always do, Viper. I'm the only one who stands a chance of sparring with you."

Valerie looks between us and calms. "Prove it. No work on this honeymoon. Just us, living an amazing, extravagant life together."

With Valerie, there's always a challenge, an adventure, and an extraordinary reward waiting at the end of it all. I can't wait to embrace the future we'll build together, filled with everlasting love and happiness.

Milton Keynes UK
Ingram Content Group UK Ltd.
UKHW010849280923
429557UK00001B/15

9 798223 151265